S0-BZM-183
2013

advance praise for

In Search Of

and others

"This collection is a powerful demonstration of the scope and significance of the dark fantastic. Ludwigsen is a weaver of bleakly gorgeous parables and *In Search Of* is a masterwork."

—Laird Barron,
author of *Occultation* & *The Croning*

"With his second collection, Will Ludwigsen has moved into an elite group of writers capable of dazzling prose and the kinds of ideas that make lesser imaginations (like this one) jealous. All this and he still manages to imbue his stories with an underlying wisdom about the world that is both uplifting and heartbreaking in equal measure, creating a lingering effect, not unlike a good buzz. Just as the sentient house does in the collection's fourth tale, these stories will come looking for you long after you've closed the book. Listen closely to what they say because it's beautiful, and most of all, it's true."

—John Mantooth,
author of *Shoebox Train Wreck* & *The Year of the Storm*

WITHDRAWN
DOWNERS GROVE PUBLIC LIBRARY

"Ludwigsen's well-wrought, entertaining tales feel like a mashup of Ray Bradbury and Stephen King, and his evocative, whip-smart prose steeps readers in a realism that's mordantly funny and matter-of-fact but glimmering with whimsy and horror that leaks around the edges… Ludwigsen's creepy, comic world reveals plenty about our own."

—*Kirkus Reviews*

(more praise overleaf)

"The venerable Weird Tale has a brand new practitioner. Ludwigsen's not-quite-horror, not-quite-fantasy tales are an unsettling mixture of tenderness and terror."

—Craig Laurance Gidney,
author of *Bereft* & *Sea, Swallow Me*

In Search Of

and others

and others

Lethe Press
Maple Shade, New Jersey

In Search Of

Will Ludwigsen

introduction by Jeffrey Ford

In Search Of *and Others*

Copyright © 2013 Will Ludwigsen. Introduction copyright © 2013 Jeffrey Ford. ALL RIGHTS RESERVED. No part of this work may be reproduced or utilized in any form or by any means, electronic or mechanical, including photocopying, microfilm, and recording, or by any information storage and retrieval system, without permission in writing from the publisher.

Published in 2013 by Lethe Press, Inc.
118 Heritage Avenue • Maple Shade, NJ 08052-3018
www.lethepressbooks.com • lethepress@aol.com
ISBN: 978-159021-270-7 / 1-59021-270-3
e-ISBN: 978-1-59021-431-2 / 1-59021-431-5

These stories are works of fiction. Names, characters, places, and incidents are products of the author's imagination or are used fictitiously.

Credits for original publication appear in the Story Notes, beginning on page 171.

Set in Caslon, Baskerville, & Myriad.
Interior design: Alex Jeffers.
Interior illustrations: Elizabeth Shippen Green.
Cover design: Will Ludwigsen.
Cover image: "Like a Forgotten Fire" by May Machin.

Library of Congress
Cataloging-in-Publication Data
Ludwigsen, Will.
In search of, and others / Will Ludwigsen ; introduction by Jeffrey Ford.
pages cm
ISBN 978-1-59021-270-7 (pbk. : alk. paper) -- ISBN 978-1-59021-431-2 (electronic book)
1. Fantasy fiction, American. I. Title.
PS3612.U35I5 2013
813'.6--dc23

2012045331

For Larry Hall, shaman and seer from a faraway land, unfit for this one except to spread peace and magick with my mother.

What I Found

an introduction by Jeffrey Ford

One gray autumn afternoon, yellow leaves flying in a cold wind out across the endless empty farm fields, I sat down by the window in my office and went In Search Of with Will Ludwigsen's story collection. I travelled light, not thinking I'd be gone long. Leaving behind all expectation, I packed only my desire to be entertained. What began as an intended jaunt, though, turned into a journey with all the requisite depth and adventure of the imagination that term implies. When I came to the end of the road, I looked up and noticed for the first time that night had fallen. Then I sat quietly for a while and inventoried the discoveries I'd made. Here's what I found along the way:

A treasure trove of imagery, marvelous and haunting, not to be forgotten—a dreaming greyhound racing in its sleep; a decrepit house pulling away from its foundation and moving across the landscape at night in search of the answers to its own haunting; a bizarre, recurring marionette show at the bottom of a well; children in animal masks, shouting their accumulated cruelty into the earth; a suspicious clown seen fishing; a troop of boys, venturing into the woods, not after merit badges but instead wonder; a mysterious manuscript of strange symbols and illustrations of undiscovered flora and fauna whose first word translates to *universicule*; the last real people in the world. Of course, this is a truncated list. A full one would go on for pages. I've not even touched on those images of the everyday, their mundanity rendered with a clarity that allows them to shine in my memory.

A world of characters—not villains, not obvious heroes—but people, like us, complex in their search for meaning, their desire for love, their foibles, their fears, their ability to fool themselves, and to surprise themselves with their own humanity. When in search of, the emotional moments of stories sometimes pounce suddenly and only once they've already sprung will you realize that they've been tracking you from the first word. It's the subtlety of the characters that allows for that surprise.

A writing style, clear and concise and flowing with the ability to carry, without strain, both ideas and emotions. Although I travelled far in this book, there was no place where I was brought up short by the writing or I felt the way get difficult of confused. Even in those pieces one might think the most challenging for a reader, say the title story with its panoply of "seemingly" errant ideas or "Universicule" with references to the nature of Deconstruction, the way was smooth, the path cut by a confident hand. This ease in reading belies a high level of craft, a working of the words and their order until they seem extemporaneous.

I gathered many laughs along the way. You'll find them yourself in your own journey. The main character of "A Chamber to Be Haunted" is a real estate guy who specializes in selling houses where horrible murders have taken place. Early in the story he claims he can sell anything and to prove it offers the ad he'd write to sell The House of Usher. I'll say no more about it. You can read the ad in the story. I will say I laughed out loud and still when I think of it I smile. Not just cause it's funny but for the mythic nature of the conceit of a real estate guy trying to sell The House of Usher. It's a great idea I'd never seen mentioned anywhere before and yet now that I've seen it, the connection seems eerily obvious. The irony of that makes my imagination laugh out loud.

I hadn't even been aware I was in search of her, but I found Elizabeth Shippen Green, an early twentieth-century American magazine and children's book illustrator. Ludwigsen uses her dream-like illustrations for certain stories. They have a misty, enchanted look and can evoke both peace and melancholy or both at once. They fit so perfectly I wonder if they're not the impetus for the tales. On the other hand, it actually seems plausible that they could've been waiting nearly a century to find their true text. They're a great part of the experience of the book, as are the author's notes for each story at the back.

I assure you, I found and gathered much more in this book, but don't take my word for it. I'm merely Spock waxing prosaic about the mysteries of the pyramids, not the pyramids nor their mysteries. To find them, you must go in search of through the stories. Let me know what you find.

Contents

Foreword

I'm so glad I was a kid before the Internet.

In a dark corner of my elementary school library, there was a four-foot section of books about ghosts, missing people, UFOs, and Bigfoot—that's where I went when all the other kids got books about sharks and motorcycles. I read them over and over again, believing every word. There wasn't yet a worldwide network, the shared knowledge of humanity, to contradict them.

In other words, I could still be credulous.

I searched my neighborhood for signs of gnome activity. I wandered the woods looking for footprints. I ran to the bathroom in the middle of the night, fearing but hoping I'd see a spirit from the corner of my eye. I avoided the deep end of our pool because, hey, there was no telling when my father would release the shark.

One of my favorite shows was called *In Search Of.* Hosted by Leonard Nimoy in the late 70s and early 80s, each episode covered a topic of cosmic strangeness—everything from Amelia Earhart's disappearance to the possibility of ancient alien visitation. I was terrified by the story of Barney and Betty Hill's abduction, and the floating face of Jim Jones in the Jonestown episode still drifts into my dreams.

Because this show was on television and Mr. Spock was talking and people in corduroy jackets were pontificating, I considered *In Search Of* one of the few places where I could learn how the world really worked. All they taught in school was the party line for good obedient citizens, and I wondered why nobody else but me and the producers worried about things like vampires.

The two biggest disappointments of my young life were that the Boy Scouts functioned nothing like it said in my father's 1963 Boy Scout Handbook and that all of those episodes were largely full of shit, an extended last gasp of Aquarian Age reasoning.

In many ways I'm glad that I didn't grow up to be a total crackpot...but sometimes, yes, I miss it. With every debunking, the frontiers of wonder shriveled inward in my mind.

We do live in a truly awe-worthy universe—four and a half billion years of sediment beneath our feet, the beginning of existence within reach of our telescopes—and I am grateful to have the world's knowledge available to me on a device I can keep in my pocket. But those wonders don't snuggle as comfortably with our neuroses as the human ones, do they? They don't seem sentient in quite the right way for good storytelling.

What I've wanted more than anything my whole life is a sign that someone or something interesting was telling a good story with our lives.

The last vestige I have of magical thinking is a notion I call "The Monkey's Paw God" from the W.W. Jacobs story. Our wishes and fears have a terrible tendency to become true just as they do for the family in the story but only in the most ironic ways. That sick confidence in caprice—certainly a result of my upbringing—is the one magical belief I wish I could shake instead of all the others.

There is beauty in the world and wonder, but I write about them less often than I should because they don't need the magic: the dark things do. And the only intelligent beings around to create that magic are us. We're the magic.

What am I "in search of"? I'm looking for any signs of imagination in the universe, and if I don't find any, I'm willing to create some of my own. The truth that paralyzed me twenty years ago has come full circle: you don't find magic but make it.

I hope some of these stories have magic in them, and that some of it rubs off on you.

And me.

In Search Of

Your answers, though you might not like them:

The universe began 13.7 billion years ago as a singularity of infinite density and temperature. It will expand and fragment until the fragments become singularities of their own. The grand unified theory is a lot closer to "it's turtles all the way down" than scientists guess.

The Earth will end with a bang and not a whimper.

Life is common in the universe, but intelligent life is not. What little of it exists uses neither radio nor space travel. Four percent of Earth's species originated elsewhere, arriving via meteorite to evolve here. No one has ever been abducted by aliens.

No dead person has ever communicated with a living one. Ghosts are not the spirits of the dead but cross-consciousness memories to which sensitive minds have non-chronological access. The few true psychics have this ability, though only three percent of those who claim to be are. John Edward isn't. You are, slightly.

The creature in Loch Ness was a plesiosaur, but it died in 1976 and locals concealed the carcass. No feral simian or missing link has ever been photographed. The Mayans died of a pandemic hemorrhagic fever. Atlantis was the island of Crete.

All conceptions of God are produced by the limitations of human neuroses. A true holy book could fit on an index card, but most of the words on it haven't been invented yet. Religions are clumsy metaphors for epiphany, often the result of errant chemicals or electrical impulses. Sometimes, though, they illuminate the truth just as parallax calculates the distance to the stars.

Shakespeare's audiences wrote all the plays of Shakespeare: their reactions shaped what actors remembered in each successive performance until they were finally written down. The Voynich Manuscript was an opium addict's dream journal.

Lizzie Borden did it, and her sister knew. Georg Jaffe, a Jewish immigrant tailor living in London's East End, performed the killings ascribed to Jack the Ripper before lapsing into gibbering mental incompetence and dying of syphilis. Bruno Hauptman didn't kidnap Charles Lindbergh Junior alone, but his accomplice had long since died when he went to trial. Arthur Leigh Allen was the Zodiac.

Amelia Earhart and Fred Noonan lived four days on Gardner Island after ditching their plane there, eventually dying of thirst and exposure. U-869 was attempting to defect to the United States in February 1945 when it was sunk by U-857 off the coast of New Jersey. Marilyn Monroe died of an accidental reaction between medications prescribed by two different doctors.

D.B. Cooper's skull lies beneath seven feet of leaves and loam in a bear cave in the Cascades, along with $140,000 of his ransom money. British troops hid half a million pounds of bullion in the Oak Island money pit in 1779 and recovered it in 1781. Their commander ordered the pit restored as a punishment to "traitorous colonial Wretches too greedy to pay His Majesty's due."

Of course O.J. did it.

President Kennedy was shot non-fatally by Lee Harvey Oswald but then killed accidentally by a Secret Service agent. Flushed with adrenaline, the agent slipped off the curb while rushing to the limousine with his weapon drawn. Because Oswald fired the initiating shot, the FBI, CIA, and Treasury Department steered all investigations to him.

After the September 11 attacks, Al Qaeda never again had the capability to execute an attack of similar magnitude.

Two and a half million years ago, one of your ancestors invented the spoon. You had a relative who fought at Actium. Your great-great grandmother shook Abraham Lincoln's hand and reported it was "clammy." Bernard Theerian remembered the chocolate bar your grandfather gave him in Paris on August 29th, 1944, as the best he tasted all his life.

Your parents did indeed meet at church, but only after your father locked your mother in the Sunday School room and charged her a kiss to let her escape. Years later, your mother only relented to his charms for rides along the seashore in his new white MG.

Your father wanted to be an architect but stopped trying after a rejection from the Rhode Island School of Design. He majored in Sociology instead because everybody was hoping to change the world back then. He drew houses on napkins the rest of his life. Your mother wanted to be a botanist but flunked organic chemistry.

Neither wanted children.

Theresa never wanted to be your big sister, and she resented your parents for making her raise you. Once while babysitting, she prayed tearfully that you'd just die. She felt terrible about it for the rest of her life.

Buddy forgave you for yanking his tail that time in the pool. A boy named Damon Phillips stole your bicycle in the fourth grade, but he took better care of it. The angry old man living across the street wasn't a Nazi but a Russian; he did poison Pippi for sniffing around in his garden, though. The fat girl at your summer camp killed herself the next fall.

Your parents knew that you borrowed the magazines they kept under their bed.

Heather Duncan would certainly have gone to the ninth grade dance with you. That gangly hick with the bad moustache who spit tobacco on you at the pep rally is on Death Row. You could have gotten another hundred points on the SAT if your mother had breast-fed you in your infancy.

Your guidance counselor confused you with another student when she advised you to work toward an exciting career in computers. You would have been terrible at it if you'd tried. Careers for which you were better suited were counselor, attorney, or teacher.

Theresa would also have been an excellent teacher. Her last memories were of spooking her little brother while watching episodes of *In Search Of* together in the basement.

Your teachers didn't know how to help you, after. Mister Bailey didn't realize that the D in Physics would ruin your university scholarship. Dean Findley thought a military school would help, but your parents couldn't afford it. Everybody knew you broke the office windows.

Meeting Lieutenant Vercek at the career fair saved your life.

Over the course of your career in Homicide, your work resulted in the arrests of six hundred and twenty people. Two hundred and fifty-four were guilty but exonerated. Ninety-six were innocent but convicted anyway. Of those, forty-four were guilty of other crimes. Only thirty-one percent served their entire terms in prison. Of those released, more than half killed again.

Jacques Hermann didn't kill those girls. You were right that Vernon Gene Johnson hid Sandy Berensen within view of the nursery window; her body was floating about three hundred yards away in an old septic tank and finding it would have clinched the case. Ervin Mitchell kept the photos of his rapes under the carpet in his father's doughnut truck for which you never got a warrant. Those garbled tapes discovered in Francis Shenck's cabin were recordings of his victims' tortured screams for his later fantasies. Gary Thorton still wants to eat you.

You arrested more black men than any other race or gender, but you couldn't help it.

Two people vowed to kill you over the course of your life. Neither could have done it. Francis Shenck's daughter was a terrible shot, and Gavin Drummond forgot after the third grade.

Sharon's parents never liked you as much as they did her last boyfriend. They took them both to dinner when you divorced. She is happy now but she doesn't regret marrying you. Sometimes she misses those lazy summer naps and midnight trips to Krispy Kreme.

Your daughter lost her virginity in your favorite chair with that dorky drum major. She made him wear his hat. Your boss's boss thinks your last name is Gilbert. That UFO you saw in the mountains was a Russian satellite burning up on reentry. The creepy man you saw at Disney World wasn't a child molester.

The man at whom you shot the bird for cutting you off in traffic on December 16, 1996, was on the way to his wedding. The dent in your rear fender from August 2001 was inflicted by an uninsured college student who couldn't afford to repair the damage. Six times in your life you have eaten fast food tainted with the body fluids of bitter service employees.

Sixteen across on the *USA Today* crossword puzzle from August 3, 1991 was "ibex." All your mother really wanted for Christmas was a subscription to *Vanity Fair* instead of all those cheese platters. You routinely used the word "flammable" when you meant to say "inflammable."

No one could ever love you enough, but Jennifer Harris came the closest. She still thinks about you and your kiss beneath the pier on prom night.

Your greatest strength is your desire to ask all the big questions. Your greatest weakness is your fear of asking the little ones.

Theresa lies face down in a grave near the 165-mile marker on Interstate 95 in South Carolina. Her murderer, a councilman for nearby Florence, chuckles when he drives his Cadillac Escalade past her grave. His only motive was convenience, and there was no way you could have caught him.

Nothing you've done would disappoint her.

Illustration by Elizabeth Shippen Green

Endless Encore

At least she still comes to see me, the little girl in the white and lavender dress—some people would have left me behind to get help.

Every day in what I assume is the late afternoon, when the sun is far enough to the horizon to cast the edge of the well in shadow, she comes. All I can really see of her at first is her silhouette, the eclipse of her small head and dangling curls against the light. From so far down, she looks even smaller than she probably is, though her voice can somehow always find its way to me.

"Hello," she says every time. "Would you like a show?"

It doesn't do any good to say yes or to say no or to say, "Can you please go for help? I think my leg is broken." She doesn't seem to care much about how I fell down here or why I haven't left.

Whether I say yes or I say no, the puppets descend on their long strings. They're the old-fashioned wooden kind with patches of cloth and hair pasted on their flat surfaces. One seems to be a man dressed in Edwardian style with a brown-gray woolen suit and hat, and the other seems to be a little girl dressed in a white and lavender dress with blonde curls. Both wear paper fairy wings on their backs.

I know the story by heart now.

"Hello, little Lizabeth," says the man in the brown-gray suit.

"Hello, Duncan," says the girl in the lavender dress.

"Will you come walk with me?" says the man.

"May I take my puppets?" says the girl.

"Of course," he replies. "Maybe we can make a show."

The puppets' legs jerk and their arms swing, the little joints squeaking as they walk and walk. This part always strikes me as tedious for a puppet show, and I've wondered if the little girl is performing a literal time or distance. If she is, I have no idea how far or how long because neither has much meaning here in the well.

"Will you come sit with me?" says the man.

"Where?" asks the girl.

"Over here," says the man. "On my lap."

Both pairs of legs draw up and the puppets dangle a moment, maybe thinking, maybe admiring the willows together. To me, they're staring at wet stone walls furred over with moss.

"You're going to miss your sister, aren't you, Lizabeth?" asks the man.

"Very much."

"Am I wrong to suspect that you're going to miss me, too?"

"Even more."

"We won't be far, you know. Down the road a few miles in our own home, a place you're always welcome, with all the woods you could want."

"But who will come to my puppet shows? Father hasn't the time, and Mother doesn't like them."

"Lizabeth, we'll build you your own theater at Barrowgrange. A grand one, with enough room for you and all your marionettes."

The girl puppet hangs her arms and head, swinging quietly in the stale air above me. "What about you? Won't you be playing with me anymore?"

"Oh, Lizabeth!" The puppet reaches for her and she tugs away. "We can't stage plays for fairies in the well forever, you know. I wish we could. I'll miss them, truly. But when people get older, they stop climbing around dry wells and imagining fairy audiences at the bottom. Someday soon, you'll understand."

"Understand what?"

The puppet in the brown suit shakes its head slowly. "That people grow up. Me, your sister…even you. And grownups play in different ways. You won't want to play with puppets someday, just as Mary and I don't."

"I'm going to play forever." The girl puppet's arms came together as though they were folded. "I want to do one more puppet show."

"Lizabeth—"

"I want to."

"I shouldn't even be here. The preparations for the wedding—"

"You be the prince and I'll be the princess." Then, in a slightly different voice accented with a stereotypical aristocracy, she says, "'Prince Duncan, Prince Duncan, whither are you going on the day of our wedding?'"

The other puppet hangs there, doing nothing.

"'Today was the day you swore to marry me,'" says the girl's voice.

"Is that what this is about, Lizabeth? Something I said when I was a boy?" The puppet reached and this time rested his wooden hand on the other's shoulder. "Oh, Lizabeth. You're still so young. Mary and I, we—"

The girl puppet whirls on its strings and reaches for him with her woodblock arms. "Mary and you! Mary and you! Mary and you!"

The puppets tangle now, the limbs clopping together. Their strings twist and twine into one cord. They clatter on one wall and then the other before dropping into the mud beside me. The head of the man puppet seems bent back at a horrible angle, and the girl puppet rests hers on his chest.

"And they lived happily ever after among the fairies," the girl at the top of the well says. "The end."

Today's performance ends.

"Wait," I'll say, a little weaker each time, but she doesn't reply. She never replies. She only pulls away, leaving me for another night and another day with nothing for company but these rotten wooden block bones, plus two sets of human ones.

The Speed of Dreams

Paige Sumner
8th Grade Science Fair Paper Draft

Introduction

It happens all the time: you're sitting in class, listening the best you can while Mister Waters goes on and on about atoms or sound waves or whatever, when suddenly you fall asleep. Your head lolls against your shoulder and some drool oozes from the side of your mouth. Luckily, Ashley Woo kicks you in the knee to wake you up before someone notices, like Mister Waters or—worse—Austin.

What's weird is that in those few minutes of sleeping, you dream like hours of stuff. You're all hanging out or playing basketball or walking the mall while everybody else is slowly raising their hands and taking notes. They all get twenty four hours that day, but *you* get a little extra.

But how much extra?

Investigative Question

How much time can you fit in a dream?

Hypothesis

Time in a dream moves faster than time in real life, so you'll live more there. How much more is proportional to real world time.

Method

Unfortunately, Mister Waters says there's no way to measure time in our dreams. Since the whole idea of my project is that time is subjective, he says nobody could compare or repeat my results in relation to the real world.

That's where Patti comes in.

Patti is our dog, a retired racing greyhound. Her name used to be Patriot back a few years ago when all the bald, sweaty men at the racetrack used to bet on how fast she could run. She had to retire because she was a bumper, so competitive that she'd knock the other dogs in the race against the walls. She never bit them or anything—just shoved them. Like they shouldn't even be in her race, you know? Like they weren't even there.

Even though she's supposedly retired, Patti still likes to run. She's fast for an eight-year-old, too. When she sees squirrels or rabbits in our yard, she peels off after them in a big counter-clockwise circle. I guess habits are hard to break. She caught a bunny once and swallowed it whole, her jaws clopping together as the poor thing slid down her throat. We saw the little eroded bones in her poop.

Patti loves to run so much that she does it in her sleep. After I brush my teeth and crawl into bed, she jumps in too and flops down next to me, sometimes teetering over like a tree and sighing. Then, in the middle of the night, she'll dream about running and kick me awake with her twitching legs. She'll be breathing all heavy, snorting through her nose and sputtering her lips. She usually does it for a few seconds and then goes back to sleep.

Now, it turns out that she used to race back down at the Orange Park Kennel Club on their quarter-mile oval. The greyhound rescue people gave us her records, and her specialty was the 5/16ths mile race, which she usually finished in about 32 seconds. I know because I added them all together and averaged them.

Lots of dogs run in their sleep, but only greyhounds like Patti probably do it for a fixed length of time, right? She spent her whole life running the same stupid race over and over again, chasing that stick as it swung around the track. If anything is stuck in her head enough to dream about night after night, it'd be that race.

So there's my basis of comparison.

Procedure

I will measure the proportion of dream time-scrunch by doing the following:

1. Let Patti sleep, staying awake to watch her.
2. When her legs start kicking, start the timer.
3. When her legs stop, stop the timer.
4. Write down the number of seconds.
5. Repeat a bunch of times.

6. Get the average time it takes her to run a 32 second race in her sleep.
7. Divide that average sleep race time into 32 to get a proportion.

Assumptions

Because Mom made me take the dummy version of science this year so I wouldn't get "all stressed" like last year, my assumptions are probably stupid. But then, I'm only thirteen and a girl with "plenty of time to become a swan" as Mom likes to say.

My assumptions, dumb as they probably are:

1. Patti is running a standard race that takes her the usual 32 seconds and not some magical fantasy race that she wins in, like, 10 seconds.
2. Patti's legs start twitching when the race starts and stop when it stops, and she isn't flying or teleporting for any part of it.
3. The amount of time scrunchable into a dream is always the same proportion. Patti doesn't dream some races faster than others.
4. Dogs and humans have the same time-scrunch proportion.
5. Mister Waters won't be mad when I hand in this project instead of the model of the solar system he signed off on.

Results

Experiment One (February 4, 9:04PM): When Patti started to twitch, I was trying to get Lisa and Austin back together—I know, stupid—in instant messenger. I couldn't reach the stopwatch in time, so I didn't get any data. I did get them back together, even though Lisa is really only in love with herself like everybody else is.

Experiment Two (February 5, 3:28AM): Patti started kicking like crazy, waking me up. Luckily, I was sleeping with the stopwatch loop around my wrist and I clicked it right after she started. She huffed and snorted, peeling her lips back from her teeth. Then, after 6.21 seconds, her legs slowed and stopped. I wrote down the time on my algebra book cover and went back to sleep. Now that I'm awake, though, I wonder if I dreamed that she was dreaming, and the stopwatch was just measuring scrunched time in *my* dream. Drat!

Experiment Three (February 6, 7:31PM): It was my turn to help with Nannah, so I had Patti come in to help. Nannah is my grandmother, and she sleeps even more these days than Patti does and sometimes twitches in her sleep the same way. While I was spooning Nannah's oatmeal between her lips, Patti started kicking under her hospital bed which made Nannah's pills go flying all over. I put down the jar and timed her at 5.2 seconds. Then I timed how long it takes to put down the jar a bunch of times and got an average of 2 seconds, so that counts as 7.2. It took me 45 seconds to pick up all the pills, but that has nothing to do with anything.

Experiment Four (February 9, 11:44PM): Patti kicked for 6.73 seconds. She also yelped, but not an angry yelp—more like a kick ass, "You want a piece of this?" kind of yelp. Nannah must have heard her back in the guest bedroom because she kind of moaned at the same time. Maybe they were running together in their sleep.

Experiment Five (February 11, 11:44PM): Patti kicked for 6.73 seconds, and it squicked me out a little that she did it at exactly the same time as before.

Experiment Six (February 12, 12:14PM): Austin came over and we sat on my old swing set waiting for Patti to fall asleep on the grass. When she finally did, he let me take his hand and use his fancy running watch to time her for 6.88 seconds, which means we were holding hands for almost ten seconds. His smelled like soap.

Experiment Seven (February 13, 2:20AM): Patti and I were under the blanket, reading that note from Austin again with a flashlight. Well, *I* was reading the note: she's a dog. I'd just gotten to the best part, about him wanting secretly to go with me to the dance but he couldn't break up with Lisa until after she'd finished the basketball season, when Patti started to dream. I clicked the stopwatch and she stopped after 7.1 seconds. Then I read the part about my eyes again.

Experiment Eight (February 14, 5:39PM): Patti was lying on top of my dress for the dance when she started running again in her sleep, swooshing it underneath her legs. I couldn't stop her because Mom was standing there all blah-blah-blah to me about wearing her makeup. Good thing there was a clock over her shoulder so I could see that Patti wriggled for 7 seconds. Mom went on longer, but she stopped when Ashley's mom came to drive me and Ashley to the dance.

Experiment Nine (February 15, 1:51AM): I'd fallen asleep in that stupid dress when Patti started dreaming. I grabbed the stupid timer and watched it for the time it took her to finish the stupid race, 6.34 seconds. Which happens to be about the same amount of time that Austin even bothered to look at me at the dance while he was all over Lisa like they were going to be married or something.

Experiment Ten (February 15, 4:57AM): I was still up, mostly just petting Patti and crying, when she ran her second race of the night. I read somewhere that greyhounds could do eight or more races in a day, so that wasn't surprising. When she finished after 6.2 seconds, I asked her if she won and she looked at me like, "Duh, I always win." That must be nice.

Conclusions

I added up all the race times and got 60.39 seconds. Then I divided that by the number of dreams (nine) for an average of 6.71 seconds each. Significant digits, blah blah blah: because I only know Patti's real world race time to the one's digit, I've got to round that to seven. So Patti runs a 32 second race in her sleep in only seven seconds.

When I divide 32 by that, I get the proportion. We get 4.5 seconds of dream time for every second of real time.

Application

Lately I've spent a lot of time talking to Nannah. I sing to her, tell her what happened at school, read her the dumb jokes from *Reader's Digest* she used to like. She never wakes up.

Sometimes she'll kick like Patti does. I asked Dad if she was ever a runner in the Olympics, and he looked at me like I was crazy and told me no. So I have no idea where she's running or for how long. She doesn't lick her teeth like Patti does, so I'm pretty sure she's not chasing anything she plans to eat. Sometimes I bring in flowers so she can pretend she's in a field.

Even if she wasn't in the Olympics, my Nannah did a lot of other things. She was born Flora Soehner on March 6, 1940 back in Pine Falls, Minnesota. She ran away from home when she was about my age, took a train to Hollywood to be a synchronized swimmer in the movies, and met my Grandpa five years later on a trip to San Francisco. They got married a month later. She worked as a waitress, a bartender, a secretary, a Census taker, a limousine driver, and even a cop. She went to Mississippi to ride with black people, marched against some war in Washington, and even brought casseroles to hippie kids in Haight Ashbury. She wrote a bunch of poems and songs, a couple of them sung by Jefferson Airplane. I tried to sing them back to her to wake her up but it didn't work.

She showed me how to sew, how to flip an omelet, and how to throw a hatchet into a tree, even though it always took me more tries than her. I wonder if she does that stuff now in dreams, or if she's doing new and different things like piloting a spaceship or being a tigress. Whatever she's doing, she doesn't have much time to tell me what to do better here, that's for sure. If I were a tigress, I'd be too busy, too.

Mom and Dad say she won't live much longer, but they're talking about the real world. Thinking like that, none of us lives very long, right?

But you get 4.5 times as much life sleeping as you do being awake. That's four times the chances to get things right, like the lives Mario gets if you don't make a jump. You can probably even do different things, like be a ballerina in one, the President in another, Laura Ingalls in the next, and a dolphin in the fourth. All while everybody else is just getting one stupid life.

So no wonder Nannah is stretching out her life like lots of old people do at the end. We think it's a coma, but really it's a dream—one where you're doing all sorts of cool stuff you want like winning every race, catching the rabbit, hanging out with Jefferson Airplane, and getting to dance with Austin. Maybe with four times the number of tries, I can do all those cool things too.

Experiment Eleven (February 27, 11:09PM):

1. Take the rest of Nannah's pills so I can catch up.
2. Write down when I start falling asleep.
3. Live four cooler lives, hanging out with Nannah. If we need money, we'll visit Patti's dreams and bet on her.
4. Wake up and write down all the big courageous things I did.

Nora's Thing

It had rolled and tumbled, whatever it was, gelatinous and tentacled, from lake to canal to stream.

People watched from the shore, following it with opera glasses and sea telescopes. Some thought it was a squid, others an octopus, others still just a glob of fatty flesh from some aquatic animal long torn apart and rotten. It was milky and translucent with tiny red hooks lining each of its sixteen flaccid arms. Deep blue bruises speckled the skin, wrinkling in like spots on a tomato. It had no visible eyes.

According to the papers, it had drifted for weeks down from Lake Huron to Lake St. Clair and now onward. Dozens of photographs had been taken from advantageous spots on the riverbank, but the results were always blurred. Biology professors tried to snag it with nets; fishermen gave chase with their boats. Somehow, the current always worked against them and it sank just out of reach every time.

No one could tell whether it was dead or merely placidly alive and content to drift. Sometimes it got stuck in bushes along the shore or caught in dock pilings, but a few good nudges with a pole usually got it going again. Someone in Algonac reported that it made a sort of whimpering, sputtering sigh when jabbed with an oar.

It left behind a rich purple trail of something like oil. When the sun hit it right, the long slick refracted the light in all the colors of the spectrum, and you could see it stretching back toward wherever the thing had come from. No one had wanted to touch it, at least until they noticed that whenever that trail swirled in an eddy beneath an old hanging tree or a shrub crackling away for fall, the tree or shrub burst alive again with vivid and unnatural colors. The leaves turned shades of greenish-purple, and the branches took on the shimmer of silver.

So Janey and all the neighborhood kids took her dying little sister Nora to the river. To watch it, of course, from a safe distance as they told their parents. To stand in the shallows with their cuffs rolled up. Only that. Just to watch.

Little Nora did not get out much in her condition, lungs always full of fluid and shivers always flexing her arms and legs. She'd rather have taken the opportunity, rare as it was, to crawl in the sand or play in the grass, but Janey held her shoulders tight and they stood together in the chilly water.

Paul and Ben ventured out the furthest; they'd been the ones Janey asked first, the ones who'd agreed to her plan. At first it was a stunt to them, but then they had to help carry Nora out to her red wagon for the journey to the river, and they'd had to catch her when she lolled to one side and then the other. She'd been too weak to hold herself up, almost as boneless as the thing in the water.

They watched the river flow, the little waves surge over the sand and into the grass. They stared at the promontory fifty yards upstream, and it wasn't long before the floating thing lazily spun around and came toward them.

Something made Janey sick to see it. It had gotten tangled in ropes and netting now, and a long plank bobbed alongside. Along its journey, it had picked up the trash of the river, and Janey didn't think that it deserved that, to gather our trash. Watching it now, she had a sense of its strangeness, its otherness, and it didn't belong here rolling in a knot of human flotsam.

"Here it comes," Ben said, flexing his fingers and rocking on his feet. He did that on the pitcher's mound in the park. He wasn't good at standing still.

Paul bent a little beside him, ready to pounce. "Ready?" he said.

Janey stared while Nora squirmed beneath her grasp. Should they even be doing this? Was it dangerous? Were they dangerous to it?

"Ready?" Paul asked again.

Nora let out a tiny cough and a big shudder, and Janey knew.

"Ready," she said. "Now!"

The children rushed into the water in a great cloud of spray. Frances stomped in huge strides, and Irene waded forward with the hem of her dress in her hands. Ben and Paul were swimming now, just swimming for it, their arms flailing wildly and their feet kicking. The noise was incredible; they shrieked and the water roared and the people on the shore screamed for them not to do it.

Paul had the longer arms and he reached the thing first. He grabbed the plank and treaded water to spin the creature around, and it swept closer and closer to Janey and Nora. So near now, they could smell its rot, something between peat loam and copper; the strange sharp tang of it seemed to pour down the backs of their throats.

The creature hung limply in the water, just three feet from Janey and Nora, who was crying. They hadn't told her the plan, and now that they were close, it was obvious that they were going to make her touch it.

But where? Janey hoisted her sister under the arms and thrust her toward the creature, trying not to cry. The odor was horrible now, and the slick of blood or poison or whatever it was had started to swirl around them.

Nothing happened.

Something had to happen. Janey wasn't going back to the shore until it did. So, eyes clenched from the spray, she lifted her sister into direct contact with it, letting her arms and legs squish into its bruised-tomato skin like some terrifying hug. Nora screamed now, and Janey wished she could clench her ears shut, too.

Four of the tentacles weakly coiled around Nora, and Janey knew she'd made a mistake. She yanked again at her sister, but the flesh only squeezed her tighter.

"Get her!" Janey shouted, and the children tried to peel the fleshy arms from around Nora. They couldn't even get their fingers in, and they all gasped as the creature made a slow roll with Nora and held her beneath the water.

"No!" Janey cried, pounding her fists on its exposed back, pounding and pounding. The others pounded, too, and Ben flipped open his pocket knife. Good, she thought, cut it open. Please. Get her out.

Before Ben got the chance, though. the thing completed its rotation, exposing a choking Nora once more to the sun. Janey grabbed her sister roughly and this time, the creature let her go, its arms draining from her sides. A whimper, very faint, came from somewhere above the surface.

With Nora in her arms, Janey kicked off from the creature and made for the shore, kicking frantically, screaming for help. The other children drifted back from the creature and let it go on, now with none of that slick substance trailing behind.

It bobbed a little, shuddered, and now the sixteen arms flowed behind it like a woman's hair. That's how it drifted the rest of the way through the canals and streams, the limbs torn away by rocks and the flesh nibbled away by fish, until it dissolved to nothing somewhere far away.

Nora lived a long, long life after that. She never coughed again, certainly. She never shivered, either. Her body grew strong and her mind stronger still. She had strange dreams for the rest of that long life, though, dreams of places and things that she later tried to paint and write about. She was famous for a time, lauded for her wild imagination, but she rarely talked about the source of her vision. When she did, she only said it was her "responsibility" to show us what she had been shown.

She held strange jobs and voiced strange opinions and never let anything bother her, not anything small. And to her, it was all small and wondrous.

Nora is missing now, escaped from an assisted living facility in this, her 110th year. There's a river nearby and a sea not far from that, and it isn't hard to imagine that she could gracefully dive in and go anywhere she wanted.

Remembrance is Something Like a House

Every day for three decades, the abandoned house strains against its galling anchors, hoping to pull free. It has waited thirty years for its pipes and pilings to finally decay so it can leave for Florida to find the Macek family.

Nobody in its Milford neighborhood will likely miss the house or even notice its absence; it has hidden for decades behind overgrown bushes, weeds, and legends. When they talk about the house at all, the neighbors whisper about the child killer who lived there long ago with his family: a wife and five children who never knew their father kept his rotting playmate in the crawlspace until the police came.

The house, however, knows the truth and wants to confess it, even if it has to crawl eight hundred miles.

The house isn't stupid, of course. It knows that leaving in the morning when that middle-aged lady strolls across its overgrown lot would attract attention. So, too, would leaving at any other daylight hour, even though by then most of the neighbors have gone to work. A beginning is the most noticeable time of a secret journey.

The house is patient. It's waited three decades and it could probably wait another three, though it isn't sure if people live that long, especially *its* people. They seemed upset and harried when they left everything behind but what fit in their arms, and that can't be a healthy way to live. The Maceks could well be dead but the house doesn't think so. It doesn't feel so, either.

At dusk the house decides to leave. Shadows from the rotting trees conceal its departure, though it isn't auspicious: the house shudders its frame and groans forward two inches. Afterwards, exhausted, it sighs through its yawning windows and leaking attic with a wood-filtered moan.

Then it tries another two inches, and another two after that. They get easier, once the house gets some practice and learns just how to tighten the posts and shuffle forward.

In the coming weeks, the walking lady doesn't notice the house is moving. She just changes her path to compensate, not even realizing she's doing it, until one day she stops coming around at all. Maybe she goes back to work or finds a brighter place to walk. Maybe she just gets a bad feeling about the lonely house in the woods, some chill that it was almost alive. The house gets that a lot.

With no witnesses, the house picks up speed and moves ten feet an hour on level ground during the daytime and even faster at night. The breeze passing through its dormers and eaves exhilarates the house, and sometimes it doesn't care if anybody sees its shadow crossing the rising moon.

~

The house keeps to the woods and meadows between properties because it wouldn't do to be found and restored. You can't go all the way to Florida with a family of four living in you, the house likes to say to itself. The house has lots of wisdom to impart but nobody to whom it can impart it like a newer house or even a shed.

For instance, it would like to tell someone that traveling in the wilderness is risky. Sometimes the weather is bad and you slip down a hillside in the mud. Sometimes your shingles get scraped away by low-hanging brambles. More than once, raccoons tumble down the chimney or through a window to nose through food the Maceks left behind. The house tries to shimmy in a scary way, thumping the old black-and-white framed photos on the wall, but the raccoons don't seem to care. They pull away a fuzzy rotten chicken bone or a green roll while the house glowers.

When it rains, water seeps through the grey insulation and bulges in big lumps in the ceiling. Sometimes one will burst, splattering plaster and moldy water across the carpet. The house winces when this happens and tries to stick closer to the trees for shelter.

~

The house waits beside highway 61, wondering how it will ever get across. A car passes every few minutes, just enough to make a foot-by-foot march across the pavement risky.

The house squats by the side of the road, watching for the darkness to come. When it finally does, the house crosses the first two lanes of the road as best it can, rattling its windows and cracking its siding to all but gallop to the median. There it rests, hoping to look inconspicuous—like someone just built a house in the middle of the road, or like the state is preserving a historic building by running the highway around it.

After the house has caught its second wind, it begins to cross the other lanes. Just when the dotted white line exactly bisects it, light fills all its easterly windows.

The house panics, though it isn't easy to tell: only an architect could see the corners go out of plumb and the walls buckle like that, though he or she wouldn't believe it.

Behind the windshield, the truck driver doesn't seem to believe it either. He blinks, screams, and veers the truck into the other lane. The steering wheel shudders in his hands as the trailer skids.

The house, not ready for 60,000 pounds of truck to crash through its timbers, shuffles as best it can to the other side. There it watches the wheels catch, lock, and then thump back onto the highway as the driver gains control again. The trailer totters left and then right, but the only likely casualty is the driver's heart rate. Probably the house's too, if it had one.

The house hates fences, especially the barbed wire ones. It has broken through many a wooden rail fence with relative ease, but the barbed wire ones drag behind the house for hundreds of yards. The house then has to gingerly slither across the wire to leave it behind, losing sometimes minutes or hours.

Probably fifty or sixty people have broken into the house since it left the foundation. The house grumbles at the lost time, but sometimes visitors are nice, especially when they leave. Some of the kids break bottles and light bulbs, and the house doesn't appreciate that. Sometimes they take things, a couple of portraits or an old fork or some other souvenir of that "creepy shack in the woods." The house wishes it could stop them, but it already has one big job to finish.

Bums rarely stay the whole night. They'll nap a few hours on a bed and root around for some liquor but then something calls them back outside—maybe a train whistle or an unfinished mission or an unpaid debt. Whatever it is, the last thing those guys seem to want is a house. Which is good because the last thing the house wants is a bum.

Nine couples have made out on the old moldy couch, green water squishing between their fingers from the cushions as they press together. The house remembers when Mr. and Mrs. Macek did that once when the couch was clean. They both were drunk on gin and tonics and she started it by unclasping the right shoulder of his overalls. The kissing kids aren't as smooth—they just shove each other on the couch, grope awhile, and then go straight to the thrusting.

Rivers and creeks are a mixed blessing. They're difficult to cross, but the current can take days or even weeks off the journey if the house navigates them right. It still floats more or less, though water washes in through the front door to the back, leaving behind silt and weeds and even flopping fish.

The house has never seen a waterfall, but it imagines one would be bad news.

In North Carolina, the house has interesting visitors: two boys and a girl, early teenagers, sweaty and sunburned from a summer vacation spent running all over the wooded mountains.

The house can tell they're adventurous, like the Macek children were before Mrs. Macek took them away. Still, they're respectful—climbing in through the kitchen window, yes, but only one already shot out by a drunken hunter.

They walk around, peeking into the stove at Mrs. Macek's forgotten roast and flipping through the stack of brittle newspapers by the green chair. They talk about the big mystery, what had happened to the people inside.

"They left so much behind," says the girl. They call her Amanda, the house discovers.

"Look at this," says the bigger boy, Michael. "There's still food on the table."

Not much after so long, of course, just scattered pebbles of dried corn and black circles where rolls used to be. Muddy animal tracks speckle the table.

"It's like the Marie Celeste," says the smaller boy with the big eyes, Jeremy. "Lost at sea, adrift for months."

You don't know the half of it, rues the house to itself.

"You think they got killed?" asks Michael, the one who keeps looking at the girl when she bends over the tables and shelves. The house doesn't appreciate him at all.

Neither does Amanda, it seems. She catches him staring and says, "Stop it." Then she turns to the smaller boy. "There's no sign of it. No blood or anything, at least."

"Maybe they were poisoned and they crawled outside, choking on arsenic to die in the yard or something," says the smaller boy. The house likes his insight: yes, the Maceks had been poisoned and crawled out all right. Just not by arsenic.

"Good theory," says Michael, punching him on the arm.

Amanda spreads out the newspapers on the table, the ones Mrs. Macek saved after Mr. Macek's arrest. After half a century, those lurid headlines crackle on the yellowed paper as the kids gingerly turn the pages with pinched fingers. Amanda reads them aloud, probably because Michael can't read. He looks the type.

"*Local Girl Missing for Three Days*," reads Amanda. The house remembers that, all right. Policemen walking the streets, swinging their lights from one side to the other, calling out her name. Women gathering in clots on each corner, whispering with their hands held to their mouths. Cub Scouts crawling in the bushes. Teenagers in trucks rumbling by late at night, chuckling over their dark jokes.

The house, of course, could do nothing to help.

Jeremy reads the next: "*Body Found in Crawl Space by Detectives.*" That actually wasn't true. A police bloodhound named Jenny dragged Kathy Henderson's bludgeoned body out from under the house while the detectives gaped. The dog pulled and pulled, and the house wished someone would just help, would just break through the rest of the rotten lattice to get her out. But they all just stared, and of course the house could do nothing.

Mrs. Macek fainted on the porch. Mr. Macek had a lot of questions for the police, but they didn't speak Polish. Not that they were listening anyway.

"*Foreign Handyman Arrested*," says Michael. He would pick that one, wouldn't he, the article with the picture of Mr. Macek being dragged from the house in his grey overalls, squinting in the flash bulbs, wincing as cops twisted his arm more sharply than they had to? There were lots of boys like him back then, too. They just happened to be wearing uniforms.

The house remembers the casseroles brought for Mrs. Macek and her children right after the arrest, the offerings of neighbors who didn't believe her husband could do such a horrible thing.

"*Immigrant Pleads Not Guilty to Child Murder*," crows the next headline in Michael's voice. "Dude looks crazy." He sidles closer to Amanda, but she sidles just as far away. "The kind of guy who'd kill a girl and stuff her under the house."

"*Crazed Handyman Offers Garbled Defense at Trial*," whispers Jeremy.

The house remembers, too, how the casseroles came fewer and fewer, stopping altogether when the autopsy photos were shown. The Macek daughters came home from the park crying, and the Macek boys came home from the baseball diamond angry.

Amanda doesn't have to read the last one: *Guilty*. It's from August 9th, 1938 and nobody bothered to cut it from the newspaper like the others. The kids can read advertisements for $50 refrigerators if they want to, but they're all just staring at Mr. Macek's horrified expression instead.

August 9th, 1938—the day Mrs. Macek, mortified by her husband's guilt and their neighbors' reaction, ordered the children to take whatever they could carry and stuff it into the car. The day they left everything behind, not just dishes and pictures but questions, too. The day the doors clattered, the lights dimmed, and the house was left to itself.

"Cool!" says Michael. "It's a Kill House!"

The house hates to be called that.

"I wonder where he did it." He looks around, grinning. "I bet there's a ring of blood still in the tub."

He leaves to go check and Amanda follows.

Jeremy squints at the newspapers and says to nobody, "Wait. These newspapers are from Ohio."

He follows his friends, silent now as though afraid to wake up the house, and steps gently down the hallway, looking into each of the bedrooms. Blank patches on the yellow wallpaper show the ghosts of pictures fallen from the walls.

The first bedroom looks like three boys shared it, two in bunk beds and one in his own. Their dresser drawers are still open with pants and sweaters spilling out of them, and metal toy soldiers lay wounded on the floor. Jeremy picks one up but then puts it back.

The second bedroom seems to have been for the girls of the family, two of them if the beds are any sign. They'd left everything behind like their brothers had: a few drawings from school hang crookedly above one bed, and a bundle of letters tied in a pink ribbon rest on a nightstand beside the other. The letter on top has the print of someone's lips. Amanda holds it up and sniffs it.

In the master bedroom, the blankets are thrown back from one bed but the other is still made. An old clock has wound down, dying three minutes past eleven. An oval dresser mirror leans away from the wall, its left half broken away. Rusted hairpins lay beneath. A closet door swings from one hinge. Metal hangers dangle between coats and dresses with ragged sleeves.

Michael leans over a nightstand to pick up a wallet. It's the one Mr. Macek had taken from his overalls when the police came. He flips it open. It has long ago been emptied of cash, but he grins and slips it in his pocket anyway.

"What are you doing?" asks Jeremy.

"I'm just taking a little something away, that's all. A real-life murderer's wallet."

"You can't just take that."

"It's not like he'll need it. Guy's long been executed."

The walls of the house creak as though resisting a heavy wind. Through the windows, however, the leaves hang motionless.

"Put it back." Jeremy points, his finger shaking.

"It's like robbing a grave," says Amanda from the doorway. "It isn't right."

Michael laughs and steps backward. He jumps up onto a bed and spreads open his arms. "You gonna take it from me?"

The house wishes the ceiling hadn't already collapsed above him some half a decade ago.

"Come get it, Amanda," Michael says, swaying his hips.

Jeremy and Amanda trade glances and frown. Then they both step forward.

The bed creaks beneath Michael's weight as he bounces on his heels. The tired wooden frame finally gives way and he falls backward to the floor, crunching on broken glass. He groans though he isn't cut. The house had hoped otherwise, but then it realizes that it doesn't want to carry a corpse to Florida.

Jeremy pulls the wallet from Michael's hand and sets it back into the dustless square on the nightstand while Michael staggers to his feet.

"I could be dead," he whines. "Stupid kill house."

Neither of his friends say anything. Quiet and maybe embarrassed, they return to the kitchen and climb back out through the window.

Michael stomps the faucet before slithering through.

The hardest thing about crawling across the country is keeping plumb. Even if you're a good 1921 Craftsman-style bungalow, your beams and crosspieces will be torqued to their limits over all that terrain in all that weather.

Tornadoes hit in Georgia, some forty years after the house leaves Ohio. By now, the house is gray and its siding curls at the ends like a dead man's fingernails. The wind, green with stolen earth, blasts through the broken windows and tears the curtains away. Moss on the roof peels from the corner like a scab before tumbling into the vortex.

The hail rattles against the roof. The rain shoots sideways through the door. The newspapers dissolve. The couch bloats.

With nowhere for the wind to grab hold, the tornadoes move on to more satisfying victims. They wobble away, leaving the house bewildered in the middle of a field.

The house gathers its wits and crawls away through the broken branches, onward to Florida.

There aren't houses like this house near Fernandina Beach, and you'd think it would be embarrassed. It isn't. The clean adobe houses in the retirement community are full of Formica and fiberglass, slathered pink and teal with concrete seashells hanging by their doors. They've never had a baby born inside. They've never seen a really good teenage argument or a night of gin spilled in the master bedroom. Their pastel walls flicker with reruns.

The house sticks to the woods on the edge of the development, circling from the north and sensing the last of the Macek family, the commander of the toy soldiers, Julian Macek.

Of course he likes to walk still, young Julian. He always liked it back in Ohio, even in the middle of the night. He'd sneak out of his window and patrol his town like an amateur watchman. Of course he still does that today, eight hundred miles and seventy years away.

Now he carries a broom handle walking stick. He's driven a finishing nail headfirst into the end, just the thing for spearing a paper cup or an attacking animal's eyeball. He shakes it much like his father did at the kids who rush past his house on their bicycles and skateboards, not quite sure if he's missing something important and American.

The house watches Julian on his daily patrol. He follows the walkways through the golf course though he does not play. He squints at the other old men in their plaid hats and white shoes, sometimes raising the broom handle at them in either salute or warning. They chuckle and wave back.

The house realizes that it has never thought of how to call attention to itself. On windy days, you can hear the groan of rotting joists and the whistle of split shingles, but the air is stagnant during the Florida summer and the high drone of locusts would conceal them anyway. It can't whistle or snap its fingers, and houses can only whisper to their occupants.

After a week of waiting fifty yards off the seventh hole for Julian Macek to get a funny feeling on the back of his neck, the house decides to risk everything and just edges its corner onto the fairway.

Julian Macek sees it first one rainy morning. His broom handle clunks upon the concrete but stops about thirty feet from the house. He stoops, peering past the pine trees and curving palms at the leaning wreck, more snail than house.

Julian looks over his shoulder to the left and then to the right. He steps across the grass and touches the corner. A charge crackles along the old cloth-sheathed wiring.

Come inside, the house wants to say.

Julian limps around the house, examining every side: the missing back steps, the jagged windows, the wavy porch planks. The house waits and hopes for any sign of recognition.

Julian staggers back, holding his hand over his mouth. He bends gasping toward the ground while the house worries.

I traveled a long way, the house wants to say. Come inside.

Julian's face is white, but he steps onto the porch and tries the door. The last few months of humidity and vibration have finally rusted away the tumblers in the lock. The knob falls into Julian's hand and the door swings open.

Come inside.

Julian, holding his broom handle like a spear, walks into a living room he last saw over his mother's shoulder. He grimaces at the kitchen table. Cans and candy wrappers crunch under his feet as he shuffles from one room to the next.

In the master bedroom, he picks up his father's wallet in his shaking hand. He opens it, sees the Ohio license, and then drops it to the floor.

He runs now through the house, crashing into one wall and then the next, clutching his narrow ring of white hair. He drops his broom handle in the hallway. He slips on the mold-slick carpet and crawls the rest of the way from the house.

Wait. Wait.

Julian Macek, the son of a convicted and executed child murderer, scrambles for his life from his childhood home.

That's not the way it was supposed to go at all, thinks the house. Confession turns out to be harder than it expected.

The house has a speech prepared, though it has no way to deliver it. "We're brothers, you and I," it would like very much to say. "Maybe we both crawled to get here, but we're both still standing. We wouldn't have made it this far carrying the things we know if your father hadn't done a good job. He was for building things, not destroying them."

But eloquence doesn't come easy to a house when all its words are only architecture. There's only so much to say by standing still, by still standing.

Just as the house resolves to finish the journey and crawl the quarter mile to Julian's backyard, a flashlight beam bobs over the fairway, coming closer. Julian, a bottle in one hand and the light in the other, cracks his knees against the porch and curses. He totters back and walks up to the door.

"I've spent my whole goddamned life running from you, and now here you are," he says, narrowing his eyes to focus through the dusty glass.

You didn't have to, the house wants to say. That's what I've come to tell you.

Julian can't hear it, of course. He stomps into the house, crunching across a fish skeleton from somewhere in Kentucky. He glares down at it confused. Then he stops at the doorway of the room he shared with his brothers, dead twenty years ago. He bends to the floor and picks up one of his old soldiers. Clutching it in his fist, he continues to his parents' bedroom.

There he sways, staring at their beds.

"I watched everything I did, just in case," whispers Julian. "I stayed away from children, even my own, just in case. I stayed away from girls. I married late, too late. I yelled and fumed to let out whatever he might have given me. All I wanted was to forget him, but here you are to remind me."

It was me, the house wants to say.

"Is this like the mystery stories? The scene of the crime comes back to visit the criminal?" Julian stamps his foot and pipes clank against the beams.

The house tenses, hoping he'll hear, hoping he'll do it again if he doesn't.

"They already got him," shouts Julian. "Are you happy?"

No, thinks the house. I killed her.

Julian shatters the bottle against the wall and vodka soaks into the yellowed wallpaper. He watches it, considering. Then he stoops and flicks open a lighter. Flames crawl up the wall.

Julian's father built the house almost entirely from wood that came on a truck as a kit from Sears. Niklas

Macek, a skilled carpenter, carefully fitted each piece to the other and nailed them square enough to travel eight hundred miles further than any architect had ever imagined.

Fire scurries from joist to joist and beam to beam while the insulation smolders. Paint bubbles on the walls in streaks. Plaster crumbles and furniture flares. The house holds together.

Julian stares at the empty squares where the family portraits once hung. Mama died soon after the move. Anja and Maria left as soon as they could, marrying the first cretins they met hoping to start better families than their own. Theodore ran away to the war, and Peter was spacey and silent the rest of his life. They're all dead now.

The house can't get away, even if it wanted to, not with fire to spread like typhoid anywhere it goes. It can't just die, either, not yet, not with Julian still mistaken.

The house inhales. Hot air flows up to the attic and cool air sucks in through the broken windows. It has no lungs or voice box, but the fire itself will have to do. Maybe a ten penny nail shrieks from two boards prying apart or expanding gases split an ancient rusted pipe; all the house knows is that it manages a single scream—one very much like Kathy Henderson's all those decades ago.

The difference is that someone hears it this time. Julian spins to his left and to his right, looking for the source. Was there someone still in the house? His worry clears his mind enough so he can race from room to room to find her.

Of course it is a *her*.

Unable to find anyone, Julian lopes outside and searches around the foundations. He bends to check the crawlspace, and glowing embers barely show the pipe, black and rusty and blood-stained. Can he see?

She crawled under after a cat, the house wants to explain. One of the calicos from Mrs. Gabbard's yard. She crawled under and cracked her head. She bled all over, and I couldn't stop it. I'm sorry. It happened so fast, too fast for a house.

Julian crawls backward to escape the crashing beams and soaring sparks, and the house wonders if he understands. Blood and mud and rust look a lot alike, after all. It's a long shot, much like coming all the way to Florida in the first place. Julian does look amazed, surprised, his eyes wide. He doesn't look as slumped and heavy, at least.

Relieved, it settles exhausted into the fire and sleeps.

Illustration by Elizabeth Shippen Green

Whit Carlton's Trespasser

If it wasn't poachers on ol' Whit Carlton's property, it was Mormons. Or Klansmen burning a cross. Or a circle of chained apes escaped from the zoo. You'd damn well think that Whit had himself El Dorado on that hundred acres of his, for all the people he suspected of trying to raid it.

Sheriff Beaumont wasn't having it this time. He folded his hands behind his head and leaned back in his industrial metal chair. It squeaked as he propped one boot atop the other on his desk and said, calmly, "Now, Whit, just what *kind* of clown you reckon is on your property?"

"What *kind* of clown? What the hell does it matter?" Whit's voice had an entertaining way of leaping into the upper registers when he got excited, which was often. Truth be told, folks in town liked to "poke the bear" every so often, telling Whit they'd seen Communists taking an envelope from his mailbox or Mrs. Carlton stepping out with a Methodist.

"It matters in lots of ways, Whit. There are different tactics required for, say, your garden-variety circus clown versus your court jester or your fool. Different gauges of buckshot, too—a harlequin has tougher hide than a rhino and they get ten times as mad."

"I didn't vote for you, Beaumont," Whit said.

"Nobody did. I was appointed by the mayor." Sheriff Beaumont sighed. "What did you say this clown was doing?"

"He was fishing out in the crick, southeast corner of the property just where the cypress swamp starts up."

"Fishing."

"For the sake of Jesus, yes, fishing."

The hook passes, the hook passes, the hook passes again. It lingers near the mouth, tantalizingly close.

"What kind of bait was he using?" Beaumont really wanted to know; it was spring, and the shiners weren't as easy for the bass to see in all the sunlight. If the clown was using worms, maybe, or—

"I didn't stop to *talk* to him. I only saw him. He was perched in a tree, like, dropping his line into the water, casual like he owned the place."

"He catch anything?"

Whit Carlton's face turned as red as a match head, and Sheriff Beaumont figured he ought not to light it.

"Now, trespassin's a crime, that's a fact—whether you're a clown or not. You see any evidence that he was fixin' to stay overnight? A hobo's bag, maybe, or some blankets or whatnot?"

"I saw him and I came straight to you, Sheriff."

You ran, thought Sheriff Beaumont. Which wasn't all that odd, given how you don't much expect to see one in the woods like that.

It dances, the hook, just on the edge. The wide silvered eyes seem mesmerized by its glint and the mouth slowly opens.

"See, the reason I ask is it's a hot day and the cruiser's been acting up and we've only got one cell with the high school football game coming up. Now, if he's still there and we catch him, he's gonna take up room we'd usually use to get a drunk off the roads. You want that on your conscience, Whit, a drunk out running over cheerleaders just to put your clown away?"

"The law's the law!" Whit cried.

"I don't deny it, no sir. I'm only asking you to think of the worst thing that can happen with a clown in your back forty. The worst thing, the absolute worst, and compare it to Hap McMahon's pretty little Opal getting run down. Just as a for instance, mind you."

Whit thought that over, something he showed by clenching first one side of his mouth and then the other. "He could steal fish," he finally said.

"They your fish?" the sheriff asked. "I mean, when you think about it, they're really God's fish, aren't they? And if He wants to give a few to that clown in the woods, I don't know that we ought to stop Him."

"So I'm to let anybody come on my land all willy-nilly? What's the point of having it, then? You tell me that."

"The point of havin' it, Whit, is that you're a bigger man for letting folks use it from time to time. When was the last time you was fishing for food on someone's farm dressed as a clown? Never, that's when. Cut the man a break. Be a Christian, will you?"

Whit tried to say something and then stopped. He tried to say something else and stopped again. Finally, he stormed from the police station, off to scream at the old men playing checkers or one of the ladies at the bank.

That's a good day's police work, though Sheriff Beaumont, tipping his hat over his eyes.

The hook catches, slips, catches for good on her blued lips. She rises from the water on the end of her puppet string, her black hair washing back across her pale and wrinkled scalp, and he clutches her cold body close. He squeezes, even, and brown creek water oozes from the knife wounds. She's found, found again. Found. She's his again.

We Were Wonder Scouts

Yes, I was there: a Wonder Scout, one of nine, at our first campout led by Charles Hoy Fort himself in the summer of 1928. Back then, we didn't have handbooks and uniforms like you do now, no recorders or cameras. All we had was our need to see more than everybody else, to uncover the realness behind things. During that trip to the Adirondacks, we saw something real, all right, something terrible and even wondrous. It's probably saved me from a life of...whatever it is that most people lead.

I was thirteen then, the son of Norwegian immigrants living in Queens, and I needed saving. I've come to respect my father and my mother in the years since, just like you will, but back then they seemed so needlessly grim and unimaginative...just like yours do. Father had earned his way to America with fifteen years of wet freezing misery on the sea, and he never let anyone forget it, least of all me.

"Your mother waited for me, Harald, you know that?" he'd say. "I worked those ships for fifteen years, but she knew I'd come back. She knew I'd come for her. But I had to earn it first, and you have to earn it, too."

"Earning it" meant going to school at I.S. 25 every day, paying attention, doing my homework, and coming home to my father's newspaper stand in the afternoons to sell *The New Yorker* and Pall Malls to men taking trains home from Manhattan. I wasn't allowed to read the scientifiction magazines because then we couldn't sell them. Or so he said.

My parents, Father especially, had little interest in the imagination. "Why would you read things that someone else made up?" he always wanted to know. We had no books of fiction in the house or a radio, and I didn't have many toys.

What I had was Thuria, and it was better. In the shadowy crawlspace beneath my house where only I could fit, I built a kingdom out of discarded sardine tins, thread spools, and cereal boxes. A wide boulevard wound between four hills to a colander capitol dome. There, King Wemnon and his twenty wise councilors benevolently discussed and executed their national affairs. Sometimes they called the men to arms to repel giant invading animals, usually the neighbor's cats. Often, they built elaborate fortifications along the frontier to defend against the evil Count Pappen and his massing armies. At least once, they sent lone heroes across the dusty wasteland to rescue poor Princess Annabella from the Tower of Eternal Woe.

A strange sensation of stretched time would overtake me when I visited Thuria, started by a sort of whispering trance, and I could perform whole epochs of its development in just a few stolen moments before dinner. Have you ever felt that way? It's a feeling of total absorption, the kind that seems to hum and fizz against the edges of your brain.

But all great civilizations have their end, and Thuria was destined to be no different. One evening after work, my father saw my shoes poking out from underneath the house and he pulled.

"We didn't come all the way to America just for you to imagine somewhere else," he said after he looked inside. He got the broom and, with the same caprice as the sea washing over Atlantis, he swept Thuria into history.

"The only life you need is yours," he told me, with the tone of someone doing me a favor.

Now, I've lived a long time since, and I can tell you that it wasn't a favor. I've never felt the absence of a person as much as I've felt the absence of Thuria. I fell sick for almost a week after its destruction, shivering beneath a blanket in my room despite my mother's care. When I returned to school, to the bullies who chased me through the hallways and yelled "hurm-hurm-hurm" to make fun of my accent, I hunched at my desk all day staring at math problems and maps of dull places. When I returned from school, my feet fell hard onto the sidewalk like I wore shoes of iron. My dinners were bland, my baths were cold, and everything seemed as yellowed as an old picture.

I might have grown into a different man that way, the kind who skulks and flinches his whole life, who talks at parties about what roads he drove to get there, but then I found Mr. Fort's poster at the library on Fifth Avenue and everything changed.

As far as my father knew, I spent my afternoons studying English, and that wasn't entirely wrong: all the books about castles and ghosts and heroes I read in the library were certainly written in English, and I studied them closely. I'm surprised that I even noticed Fort's sign at all, and I sometimes doubt it was only luck.

"BOYS! DO NOT BE CATTLE!" it seemed to shout. The handwriting shrank smaller and smaller the further I read. "What do you see from the corner of your eye? There are secrets all around us, and the vibrations of the universe are not perceivable by common senses. Do you want to see the ropes and wheels behind the facade? Then come to the next meeting of the WONDER SCOUTS!"

I'd heard of the Boy Scouts and even met a few. Maybe they're different these days, but in my school at least, they were either swaggering bullies who wanted to join the Army as soon as they could or sickly goody-goodies who organized every project like they were building the Pyramids. I'd always wanted to go camping, but it didn't seem worth it if idiots like that would be there, too.

But Wonder Scouting...well, that had the sound of something different. I did a lot of wondering. What was going on in Loch Ness? Were ghosts really the spirits of the dead? Was there ever really a minotaur? How did Stonehenge get there? Were there really mummy curses? Could someone still find Excalibur? If anybody was a born Wonder Scout, it was me.

Well, me and Mr. Fort. When I met him at the first meeting, he wasn't anything like any adult I'd ever met. Though mustachioed and barrel-chested like a taller Teddy Roosevelt, he was more a scholarly sort than a man taken with physical adventure. He wrote books about the strange things nobody noticed, spending hours reading and collating articles in newspapers from all over the world. He kept boxes and boxes of notes about snakes dropping out of the sky, airships shining lights on European cities, giants walking the ocean floor, comets exploding, the seas running red. He talked all the time like a boy in a clubhouse about what really made the world work.

"Reality leaks," he told us at the first meeting. "The consciousness that imagines us into existence doesn't always remember all the details. It gets distracted. It lets things slip. It can't keep up the illusion in all places and all times, and it's our job to find those places and times, to peel back the edges."

There were eight other boys at that meeting (we didn't have girls in the Wonder Scouts until the Sixties), and I remember them all to this day. There were Hiram and Caleb from the Bronx, twins who lived just a few doors down from Mr. Fort's house; they spoke at last year's Jamboree. There was Clarence, the boy whose father ran a bank downtown and gave him a ten dollar bill every week; he wore a suit to the park. Dudley built ghost detectors from cans and wire, nothing like the fancy EMF ones you have today. Stevie smelled like trash, and we never asked why. Petey came all covered in bruises and was the quietest boy I'd ever met, except when you asked him about alligators; he and I are still friends, long after our wives have passed on. Patrick's father worked the docks and wanted his son to learn the trade. Tony's parents came from Italy, and they didn't understand the importance of fishmen and spaceships like all of you do.

With Mr. Fort's advice and urging, we looked together for those peeling edges of reality. We weren't very organized about it—there were no formal badges for ghost hunting or cryptozoology yet, even if we'd had uniforms on which to sew them—so we just kind of kept our eyes open while we went to school or did our chores. We peered into sewer grates for tiny people. We listened at tavern doorways for the whisper of alien languages. We broke into haunted houses and rapped on all the walls, climbed over junk piles searching for misplaced Roman artifacts, spit into Mason jars to measure the proportions of our humors, and hypnotized each other with pocket watches to plumb our evolutionary memories. Just like the things you've been doing all week here at Camp Manticore.

We lived, as best we could with parents and schoolteachers nagging us to do dull things like chores and homework, by the tenets of the Wonder Scout oath. Will you say it with me?

On my honor, I will do my best
To confound the expectations of society,
To observe the super-consciousness in all its workings,
To seek independence in body, in intellect, and in spirit.

We followed the Wonder Scout Law, too, which we recited at every meeting.

A Wonder Scout is curious, adventurous, strong, observant, resourceful, brave, skeptical, thoughtful, and aware.

We only had nine back then, but you've added "careful" these days. That's fine; lawyers need work too. Mr. Fort wasn't exactly what you'd call careful, and neither were we. You didn't have to be in 1928, or so we thought until that camping trip to the Adirondacks that made me a Wonder Scout forever.

See, Mr. Fort had discovered in his research that several people had disappeared near Moreau Lake over the years from 1925 to 1928, and he figured we'd be the perfect team to investigate. We'd had some practice now with research and investigations, and there wasn't a boy among us who wouldn't notice a man's socks didn't match if we saw him across Times Square.

To one of our biweekly meetings in the library basement, Mr. Fort brought a map of the terrain for our briefing.

"That's it, boys," he told us. "See where those lines converge? Those are vertices of superluminal power, the harp strings of the Earth, pluckable only by the sensitive and the damned. When they come together like that...well, it's no wonder that people seem to disappear to common eyes."

"Are we going to disappear?" Petey asked. He's always been a little cautious, even today.

Mr. Fort wouldn't let him worry. "At worst, we'll be absorbed into the super-consciousness, learning and seeing all knowledge at once in a single stupendous flash. More likely, we'll find a tunnel to an underground civilization of pygmies or a portal through time."

"Or a sinkhole," Petey suggested.

Mr. Fort narrowed his eyes at that, I remember. "Well, if you want to buy what *They* tell you, sure. A 'sinkhole.'"

Luckily, Mr. Fort didn't bring all that up when he asked our parents for permission. It took some convincing for my father to let me go, and I'll admit I was vague on the exact name of the organization; we were boys and we were scouts, and that was all he needed to know. As far as Father thought, I was learning to tie knots and chop trees, growing big and strong and American. I didn't mention that Mr. Fort was as likely to fly to the moon as tie a knot. More likely, even.

We traveled four hours to the mountains in a borrowed school bus, and Mr. Fort spent most of it lecturing from the front seat, listing the missing people from memory. Mine's not as good after all this time, but I'll try my best. The dates are probably wrong, but they're close.

"August 12, 1925: Pauline Walters, lost while gathering blueberries. November 3, 1926: Emily Lindbergh, no relation to the aviator, lost while playing tag with her brother. April 16, 1927: Penny O'Hare, a girl witnesses saw walk over the top of a hill and then never return, vanished in thin air; the authorities searched for her with bloodhounds. June 27, 1927: Susan Franco, escaping in the night from her drunken father, never found. March 9, 1928: Mary Williams, one of her saddle shoes left behind near the roots of an oak tree."

Something struck me. "They're all girls," I said.

"Excellent observation, Harald," said Mr. Fort. He wasn't watching the road that well. Like I said, we weren't careful yet. "Do you think feminine sensitivity makes them more amenable to seeing through time and space? Or are hearty human women simply appealing to the ancient races?" He waved his hand. "Dryads and so forth?"

I didn't have an answer for that, so I shrugged.

"We'll just have to find out for ourselves, then," he said. "There's no substitute for direct research."

"What if they're dead?" Petey asked. Of course he'd think of that—he became a doctor fifteen years later.

Mr. Fort shook his head. "Where are the bodies? Where are the footprints? Where is the panicked confession of a killer? No, these girls just walked into another world."

"I don't want to walk into another world," Petey said, but only I heard him.

"Sure you do," I whispered to him. "We'll all be with you. Me, anyway." That seemed to make him feel better. Lost isn't quite lost when you're with someone else.

We arrived at Moreau Lake late on Friday afternoon, descending through a notch in the mountains to approach its narrow rocky shores. The place was beautiful then and for all I know, it's beautiful now. I haven't been back. I'm guessing they've civilized it, built up ice cream shops and hotels, made it safe and not at all mysterious. When we went, there were a handful of small cabins built around the lake, a few private houses, some rugged trails, and miles of wilderness. That's it. We had to carry our own tents, our own canned food, our own jugs of water.

You wouldn't think it to look at him in those thick glasses and tweed suit from the back of the handbook, but Mr. Fort was a decent outdoorsman. We pitched our tents on high ground, faced them toward the rising sun, tied our food bags into the trees to keep them from bears, and built our fire circle out of rocks so it wouldn't spread. By sundown, we'd cooked ourselves a hearty if messy meal of beans and franks out of an iron skillet, and we sat together on logs to eat it.

Most of us had never been camping, certainly not out in the woods like that, and there is something grand and adventuresome about eating under the darkening skies, isn't there? Food just seems to mean more. That moment, sitting there with Mr. Fort and the other boys listening to the surging songs of the crickets, was probably the first real magic of my life outside the city of Thuria. And it was with real people. My people. Just like you.

Soon after dark, Mr. Fort added fresh logs to the fire and handed out nine forked sticks, one to each of us.

"Tomorrow morning, lads, we'll be looking for the true magnetic terrain of the area, following the likely paths taken by the missing girls toward the gate or portal. I've found that dowsing rods are excellent ley line detectors, and we'll each carve our own tonight."

He showed us how to strip the twigs of bark—"for greater sensitivity," he said—and whittle the handles for perfect symmetry with our hands.

"It's a delicate instrument, a dowsing rod. Not something you clutch with your fists like a shovel. You hold it gently, letting it do all the work. Maybe the earth makes it move and maybe you do, but either way, nothing happens if you think too hard on it."

Each of us set to quietly preparing our dowsing rods while Mr. Fort leaned back on his hands and propped his feet close to the fire.

"Oh," Caleb moaned. "I broke mine."

"No, you didn't," Mr. Fort said. "Yours is just meant to be short."

After a lifetime in the city, my first night in the woods was more than a little eerie. In our neighborhood in Flushing, you could hear people talking at all hours, dogs barking, things rattling among the trash cans. Here, I heard only the great engine of the forest, rumbling at idle, waiting for us to fall asleep before roaring forward.

"Do you know any ghost stories, Mr. Fort?" Tony asked. He liked to tell us the ones his grandmother told from the old country, all about gypsies and potions and vengeful friars.

Mr. Fort turned and looked at him. "Ghost stories, my boy? They're just the gossip of the dead. What kind of damned fool wastes his heightened awareness of all time and space to come back and tell you that he loves you? Or where the family treasure is buried? Or who killed him? They all say the same things, those ghosts, none of it interesting. None of it sublime." He snorted. "The whole world is a ghost, echoing and fading from the perfect original. *We* are the ghosts."

That wasn't what I'd expected him to say at all. I never imagined that Mr. Fort was all that picky about the weird experiences he collected in all those shoebox clippings.

"Well," I said, "what's the scariest story you know?"

Mr. Fort squinted in my direction. "Oh, a good old-fashioned campfire yarn is what you want, is it? I'm not sure I've got one of those, but the scariest tale I've ever heard goes like this."

Everybody leaned closer to the fire, even Mr. Fort.

He cleared his throat. "Not long ago in one of civilization's greater cities, two young friends walked together at night in an old quarter of leaning brick buildings long abandoned. They conversed about their usual subjects, the unusual and the lost, and they hardly noticed as the brownstones beside them grew more and more dissolute and decayed, so absorbed were they in talk of faraway places. It wasn't until they turned a corner and saw the crumbled fieldstone house that they paused."

A pine cone in the fire popped and sparks splashed into the air.

"It had been there far longer than the others, maybe even to Colonial days. They stood looking at it, fascinated. One of them stood watching, fascinated by its architecture, curious about its history. The other? After just a few moments, he recoiled in horror and ran shrieking down an alley."

All us boys traded glances.

"The man gave chase to his friend, shouting for him to stop, to wait. But the friend ran for blocks and blocks before finally stumbling to a halt. He put his hands on his knees and gulped the air.

"'What happened?' asked the other man. 'What did you see?'

"'She was waving to me,' cried the friend. 'From the windows! A woman in grey, smiling. She beckoned from behind the glass. She wanted me to come inside, and I…I had a terrifying idea that she'd never let me out again.'"

I'm not sure about the others, but I shuddered. The gust of breeze from out of the woods didn't help.

"The other man shook his head. 'But my friend,' said he. 'There is no glass. There are no floors from which to wave. The building is a ruin.'"

By then, everyone had stopped whittling their dowsing rods.

"'But I saw it complete,' said the friend, 'As it was in the old days. I saw a fire within. She wanted me to stay with her, I'm sure of it. The left side of her face was beautiful.'"

Mr. Fort prodded a log in the fire with his boot.

"The other man wanted to go back to try to see it again," he finally said, "but his friend was clearly shaken so they walked home together in silence."

Nobody said anything for a long moment. Then Tony asked, "Wait. That's it?"

Mr. Fort didn't look up from the fire. "For the rest of his life, that other man would wonder about that night. Most of all," he said, even more quietly and almost to himself, "he'd wonder why nobody ever beckoned to *him*." He shook his head. "*That* is a horror story, lads."

All the other boys groaned and swatted their hands at him, but Mr. Fort's story gave me a strange chill. For all our searching and listening and reading, I had yet to see something extraordinary myself. I wondered if I ever would, but I didn't have to wonder long.

The next morning, after our breakfast of runny eggs and cold sausage, we prepared for our first excursion. We filled our canteens, unfolded Mr. Fort's maps, and marched into the woods with our dowsing rods.

We fanned out amid the brush, Mr. Fort at our center yelling directions. "Come around the tree! No, this way! Stop!" he'd shout. "To the left!" I couldn't tell if he had some intended direction for us or if he was just improvising. I was too busy tumbling headlong over rotten logs and getting entangled in the vines to notice. Clarence broke his dowsing rod in a fall. Caleb kept stopping to drink.

The day wore on, hot and muggy, and gnats buzzed around my eyes. By lunchtime, I was sweaty and tired of the whole exercise. I didn't know much about seeing magic, but I knew you didn't see it with a bunch of guys yelling in the woods. You didn't see it when you had to go to the bathroom or had mosquito bites all over your arms, either. Am I right?

So when we gathered in a circle of elms to eat our cheese sandwiches, I took the opportunity to drift away from the group and eat mine alone.

"Where are you going?" Petey asked.

"I've got to pee," I said, not quite telling the whole truth. What could I say to him? He'd kept me up half the night in our tent, talking about his vicious old man, and I'd talked to him as best I could. Now I was full of everyone, including him, at least for a while.

"Oh," he said. "I'll just be here." He sat on a boulder a few feet off from the other boys.

If I'd been a better person, I might have stayed. I just couldn't, though. I turned and climbed over ridge out of sight, and then I walked deep enough into the brush toward the protective drone of insects.

I did my business behind an oak, and I stopped to sit upon a log to eat my sandwich before going back. It gave a little beneath my weight, obviously hollow. I'm not sure why, but I stooped at one end to look inside.

The log was half-filled with a silt of rotten leaves and loam, and holes in the bark let in beams of yellowed sunshine. Among those beams, along a wide promenade of rich black soil, I saw the perfect place for a new city of Thuria, protected from my father, ready to rise again from destruction. Maybe I could never come back to see it, but at least I could always know that it was out here, growing on its own, living on no matter what happened to me.

It would take no time at all, I figured, to set up some pine cone buildings and a leafy pavilion. So I reached inside and traced streets with my finger. I built a capitol out of bark. I tipped water from my canteen in the center of town, a fountain celebrating the fallen kings of ages past.

And then I heard the crunching leaves of human footsteps behind me.

Turning quickly expecting to see Petey or Mr. Fort, I saw instead a man in brown dungarees and a white shirt watching me from the edge of the hemlocks. He seemed to be silently flexing his mouth, his eyes wide. His hair had strands of grass in it, as though whippoorwills had nested there. He was tall and skinny, his legs most of all, and he swayed on his feet.

"You find 'em?" he said, finally.

"Find who?" I asked.

"The little people."

I squinted into the log, and it seemed to stretch for miles. At the blurry edges of my vision, I could imagine the daily errands of a tiny civilization, but I knew that they were only imaginings. When I turned back, the man stood closer though I hadn't heard him approach.

"I don't see anybody," I said.

The man nodded. "You want to?"

When I stood up, it seemed to take longer than usual and my head felt as airy as that log at the end. I swayed in the clearing like one of the saplings, barely strong enough to resist the breeze. I had a feeling something wasn't right, but I couldn't quite decide what it was.

"I think I might have to go back," I said, though my words felt as fuzzy as cotton.

The man held out his hand but I didn't take it. He grunted and stumbled into the trees, weaving from trunk to trunk, ducking beneath the lower branches. I followed a few yards behind, listening for any sign of Mr. Fort and the other Scouts. I heard none.

We came to an igloo of branches thickly woven together. The man pulled aside a sheet of old green canvas and pointed inside.

"Go in if you want," he said.

The woods had gotten quiet, if that's the word for it. No, they'd gotten *slow*, as though the birds still opened their beaks to sing and the leaves still blew in the wind but they did it at a speed you couldn't quite perceive.

I bent down to look inside. There, lying upon a bed of moss, was a girl in a white dress, not much older than me. She was asleep, one arm cast above her head and the other crossing her chest. Her feet were bare, and her fingers long and pale with strange purple-blue nails. Her blonde hair had been sprinkled with flowers.

"She's my princess," he said, close to my ear. His breath was cold. "Annabella. I rescued her."

I blinked and turned to him. "Annabella? From Thuria?"

He raised his finger to his lips and reached for me with his other hand, wide and fleshy, the fingernails packed deeply with grime.

Time surged forward like a nickelodeon. I screamed and spun out of his reach. His mouth narrowed to speak and he lunged for me, but I was too fast. Jumping, crashing, shrieking through the bushes, I swam my way back to the others, not sure if he was following or not.

I all but fell out of the forest, covered in scratches. "I know where they go!" I cried, scrambling on all fours. "I know where they go!" Everyone came over to help me stand but I was swinging my arms in all directions.

Mr. Fort looked over my shoulder, back toward the way I'd come. Then he sprinted into the forest himself, and the rest of us followed. You wouldn't expect a middle-aged man to leave a group of thirteen-year-olds behind, but I think now that Mr. Fort wanted it more than we did, whatever he was chasing, whatever I'd seen. He could have scuttled atop those brambles if he had to.

When he trotted to a stop in the middle of a clearing, we caught up to him. He was staring at the ground, eyes wide, and we followed his gaze to the object of his horror.

It was an old green canvas tarp, bigger than the one that had formed the door of the hut. It was streaked with patches of brown blood, and the toe of a saddle shoe poked out from beneath.

There was no log. There was no Thuria. There was no igloo. There was no man.

We stood there, all ten of us, staring at the tarp a long time. Mr. Fort could probably have stayed there forever. We had to push our hands against him to get him to leave.

The guys helped Mr. Fort and me back to camp, and neither of us was particularly useful for packing up the tents and knapsacks. Petey and Caleb had to slide Mr. Fort into the driver's seat of the bus. After he sat for a few minutes blinking through the windshield, he leaned forward slowly to start the engine. It took us six hours to get home after we called the New York State Police, and I looked so sick when my father saw me that he sent me straight to bed.

That was the first night of many since that I've wondered just what I saw in those woods or how I saw it. The police found the other bodies, of course, though no one ever figured out who killed those girls or why they'd all been buried in white gowns. In all the questions I answered for detectives, I tried my best to describe the man who somehow entered or exited my Thuria, but I could never quite fit it all into words. I've found that the harder you work to explain something, the further it slips away. Maybe that's why Mr. Fort's books are all but unreadable.

After that, our meetings were never quite the same. Mr. Fort hadn't expected something so...expected out in those woods, and I think he was too spooked to take us on any other camping trips. Not that that stopped us, of course: most of us found other ways to get out again under the stars. Of course I did, sometimes alone, sometimes with Petey, sometimes with a few of the other guys—always to see just another glimpse of Thuria.

Of course I wanted to see it again. Wouldn't you? I've been a Wonder Scout for my whole long life, even when it's cost me, and I always will be. There's no changing that for people like us, a little blessed and a little damned.

I know some of you are waiting and hoping like I did for your moment of magic. I can't promise you'll have one, though looking at you here around the fire, I can see in your eyes that you've got a sporting chance. But you should know that there are no roads into Thuria, only out, and not all the people who take them are good.

It will come, Scouts. You can't be ready, but you can be brave.

Singularity Knocks

We warned those government men when they came, but being government men, they didn't listen.

Their kind used to come by regular with their papers: food stamps, crop subsidies, EPA inspection reports, revenue forms, Homeland Security affidavits. On and on. The last ones came with one of them little computers you carry under your arm like a book, and boy, were they proud of themselves.

You could tell it by how they rumbled up our driveway in that electric truck of theirs all smiling in the sunshine through the open windows. They could have been tourists out for a drive among us unlucky hillbillies, if it weren't for the suits.

Their contraption pulled silently to a stop out front by the porch, and the two men stepped out of their doors. The driver snapped the dust from his brimmed hat on his knee, and the other was already tapping away on that little tablet.

"Mornin'," said the driver. "Y'all the Sawhills?"

I was sitting on the porch with the boys, fanning away the heat and talking nonsense about the world. I'm the oldest living Sawhill, so I guess that makes me the matriarch.

"You don't have to talk like that to us, mister," I said. "We know town-speak just fine."

The man with the hat put it back on his head and smiled with a hint of embarrassment. "Sorry, folks. Sometimes it helps, you know, smoothe the way."

That man with the computer was lurking by the corner of our porch, holding it up and aiming some kind of camera at the eaves. He steered a pair of laser beams from one end to the other. I figured I'd let him do what he was doing if I didn't see any harm.

"Smoothe the way for what?" I asked. I knew what was coming next, what was always coming: talk of imminent domain, of making way for progress.

"Something exciting," he said, lifting up a foot onto the lowest step. "Opportunity of a lifetime."

I looked over at my boys, both of them in their sixties. I don't have to say how much older I was, though I guess it's enough to say I almost had them too late.

"I think we've had enough opportunities of a lifetime," I said.

He nodded, chuckling. "It's funny you should say that, it really is. Because I'm here to offer you a lot more than one lifetime."

Gerald didn't speak up much, but when he did, his voice came growling out of his lungs like a drowsy tiger. "Why don't you get to your point, Mr. Government?"

The man rubbed his chin. "I'll do just that. You see, Mr. Findley and I are here from the Department of Singularity Affairs. My name's Farmer, believe it or not. Isn't that something?"

"What's the Department of Singularity Affairs?" I asked. "Never heard of it."

"Y'all…you people are pretty remote so that makes sense. We made it through the First World cities first and then spread out slowly to the towns and villages. North America, Europe, Asia, South America, Africa: that was the order we went in, mostly. We're the clean-up men, if you don't mind the expression — taking in the last few stragglers."

"Taking us in where?" Gerald asked. His brother Wayne folded his arms in support, pretty much the only way he liked to talk anymore.

"The future," Mr. Farmer said. "The Singularity. It's the End of History, the Beginning of the Future. It's the birth of the human race is what it is."

Findley was walking that tablet of his around the corner of the house. If he wanted to measure the old chimney, I didn't see any need to stop him.

"You see, we've finally made it. Thousands of years of blood and struggle and we've finally evolved. Our machines do it all for us now, and work as we used to do it is dead. There's no farming anymore, no ranching, no building cars or houses. It's all in the computer now, where we all live in a simulated paradise." Farmer gestured to us grandly. "We're here to Upload you!"

"I didn't ask to be Uploaded," I said.

"When you know more, you will. Imagine living anywhere you want, any way you want. You want to live in a pre-Civil War mansion? You get one. You want to live in ancient Egypt? Pick a dynasty. You want to go to space? Whoosh, off you go."

"What if we want to sing hymns to our Lord in eternal peace?"

"Lots of people choose that, yes, ma'am. We've got them broken up by faith if you like it that way."

"So you're taking us to heaven, is that right?"

Farmer thought that over. "Well, I guess it is heaven when you think about it like that. It's what you were promised, anyway: a life of the spirit. We're saving the human race forever, storing it in memory tended for a million years by robots. When the sun goes out in six billion years, the Containment Unit will still be headed for the edge of the universe."

"What about our bodies?"

"You won't NEED your bodies, don't you see? All the pleasures of the flesh will be stimulated directly in your software."

"What happens if there's a lightning strike? Or squirrels chew up the wires like that time our AOL went out?"

"Squirrels?" He laughed. "I don't think you understand the scale of this thing. We've thought it all through, the greatest minds of the human race at the top of its game. The servers are crash-proof, impervious to all natural phenomena, and completely powered by the magic of fusion."

"If that's all true, what are you doin' here?" Gerald asked.

"We're looking for YOU," Farmer said. "We're like history's ushers, helping you out into the light of a darkened theater. 'Step this way, folks!'"

"What's it cost?"

"Cost? There's no money anymore. What's cost but someone's crazy idea of what work and time are worth? If there's no work and there's all time, then money is obsolete."

"Just like we are, it seems," I said.

"In your present forms, yes, I suppose you are. But in the New Reality, you can be cyborgs or elves or bunnies...or even good old fashioned salt-of-the-earth country folk like yourselves. Findley here is scanning up your place so you can have it if you want."

He wasn't a bad salesman as salesmen go, especially government ones. He was basically offering heaven, after all, and not even my dead husband Gerald Sr. could blow that pitch.

Farmer seemed to see what I was thinking. "We couldn't Upload your loved ones, of course. But they're in your memories, and we have algorithms to bring them right back. Not perhaps as solid as you, but...solid enough."

So that was it. An eternity of joy and happiness within the machine, spinning into the galaxy, being whatever we wanted with all the people we'd ever loved. Gerald. Grandmama. Even Rotgut the dog, I guessed. It was a wondrous proposition, no doubt about it, especially given the price on the package.

"Nah," I said. "I don't think we'll be buying today."

Farmer held up his hands, unfazed. "This happens every time with the Stragglers. You want a life you think is real and not the one you can make yourself. It's scary, living a do-it-yourself existence that goes beyond sowing and reaping. I understand. But let me cut to the chase here: you are the last. Or, more accurately, you are the SECOND to last but for Findley and I. And we want to go home to the Singularity."

"Nobody's stopping you," I said. "We'll stay out here, keep an eye on things while you're gone. Make sure nothing happens to your spaceship before it goes up."

The smile wore thin on Farmer's face. "I wish it could be so, I really do. But I'm afraid there's a security issue leaving you behind. You could interfere somehow if you changed your minds. Either everybody goes or nobody does, and you're all that's left of the everybody."

"Well, we ain't going," I said. "That's final."

By now, Findley had come around the other side of the house. The two of them stood together, eyeing us.

"I'm afraid that it is, ma'am," Farmer said. "We've got the authority to Upload you unwillingly, if necessary."

"And we've got the authority to toss you off our property." I turned to the boys. "Wayne, go get the scatter gun."

Farmer shrugged. "You'll be Uploaded by the time he gets it. The good news is that he'll *imagine* he pulled it off."

Wayne thundered into the house in his heavy boots, grabbed his pappy's shotgun, and swung it back out toward the government men. That one with the computer was aiming his lasers at us, and Gerald and I dove for cover. The beams danced across my liver spots and I brushed them away and away but they wouldn't go.

My boy pulled both triggers. The government men blasted out into the weeds, their top halves falling a few seconds later than their bottom halves. They sure looked surprised with those wide eyes and those open mouths.

"Goddamn, I hate having to do that," I said, climbing back on the porch. "How many more of them can there be?"

"Don't reckon I know," Gerald said as he watched his brother drop the two empty shotgun shells onto the porch.

"Now you better pick those up, son," I said to Wayne. "And you go double-check on those servers back in the house, just to be sure."

Settled back in my chair, I continued fanning.

Ain't one Singularity enough for them?

A Chamber to be Haunted

Sure, I could sell the House of Usher.

> *Spacious, secluded historic home on waterfront property now available for immediate purchase. Eight bedrooms and four bathrooms perfect for a growing family. Gothic charms abound: tall windows, black oaken floors, carved ceilings and archways, pre-stocked library and music room, suits of armor, hand-woven tapestries. Must see to believe.*

Poe didn't do himself any favors with the "vacant eye-like windows" or the "rank sedges" or the "black and lurid tarn." Rule Number One in the stigmatized property game is that you never call anything a "tarn."

I sell haunted houses and murder scenes for a living, places real estate agents call "stigmatized property" in a death-defying swing of the semiotic trapeze. Remember the mannequin house, where Ralph Franklin Law buried all those dressmaker dummies "for the practice" as he said? I sold that. Remember the Rockwell place, the one with the soundproofed room in the center lined with hooks? There's a happy family living there now, thanks to me; they use the room for a home theater. Remember that windowless office building downtown, the one built by those "Satanists"? That went for $1.2 million, including the gargoyle fixtures.

Selling stigmatized property is easier than you think, especially for a person trained as I am in the mutability of language. You don't spend ten years as a Deconstructionist critical theorist and college professor without learning a thing or two about how to fold a signifier back on a signified. It helps that I consider "truth" and "value" to be slippery functions of language, but then so does every other real estate agent. I just happen to have a long boring theory to prove it, one whose publication in a literary journal made me famous for about ten solid minutes before my university sent me packing. I'm told professors still hand out smudged photocopies of that article to upset their complacent undergraduates.

There's not much money in the smudged photocopy business, so I ante up in society's capitalist card game by selling houses for a living. It isn't as onerous as it sounds: I'm out in the fresh air, I meet interesting people, I get to work on my practical semiotics, and sometimes I get a decent check for my efforts.

The realty agency I work for, Austin and Prock, specializes in two adjacent areas of Jacksonville known as Riverside and Avondale, just north-ish of the St. Johns River. Both are old neighborhoods with tree-lined streets, ritzy specialty shops with no logical income, and plenty of historic architecture. We've got Tudors, Spanish revivals, lots of Prairie and Craftsman bungalows, and even a couple of imposing Greek Classicals that look more like banks than homes. It isn't the Florida you expect, all adobe and flamingoes. If you want that, you can drive ten miles toward the sea and get all you want from other real estate firms.

Many of the houses in our neighborhood were built from the early 1900s onward, and they have a lot of stories still living in them, most dull and clichéd. Dad shot Mom for sleeping around, Junior stabbed Dad for all his weekly beatings, Papa never came home from the war, Mama's first baby was a jellied husk. The trouble with angst is that there are only so many things people have angst about, mostly money and love and death. The Florida humidity soaks all that into the lathe-and-plaster walls, and sometimes it seeps out into the present.

Take, for example, the kill house on Valencia Road.

A kill house is just what it sounds like: a place where someone got murdered. It's different than a death house, which is just a place where someone died. You're probably inside a death house right now; most are. The last droplets from an old man's dying gasp might still be moist in your wallpaper. Someone's final explosive diarrhea could still be stained in your carpet padding.

See, that's why a kill house is better than a death house. People clean a kill house much more ardently than they would a regular death house. They rip out the bloody carpets, remove the gore-smeared drywall, and replace the murderer's broken entrance window with an energy-efficient double pane one. Those people on HGTV haven't done a *real* extreme makeover if they've never raked bones out from under a house.

The house on Valencia was no House of Usher, and not just because it was still standing. Normally, places like that—three bedroom, two bath Victorians situated just yards from a park—tend to go quickly in Riverside, especially with all-new modern amenities. This one even had some positive history, having once been split by a local dentist into a downstairs office and an upstairs apartment. Half the crowns in every law firm and boardroom had come from that downstairs office, and that apartment had been home to the dentist, his wife, and their daughter for nearly a quarter century.

At least until he'd been murdered with all the subtlety of a cow slaughtered by dynamite.

For that trivial reason, the Valencia house had been listed on the Austin and Prock inventory sheet for close to three years. The new owners refurbished the house and removed almost all vestiges of its former purpose or infamy, but the realtor is legally required to mention that infamy so it never sold. Plus, I'm sure a few spritzes of luminol on the upstairs hardwood floors could still provide enough glow to read by under the black light.

So I wasn't hopeful about the Sidwells, Nolan and Doris, when they asked to see the Valencia house after exhausting all the others on our listing sheet. They'd recently reached their middle age and paid off a house in the Mandarin suburbs. Now that their daughter had graduated early from high school and gone off to college, they were ready for a smaller house.

Nolan worked for a national insurance company, something with systems or management or systems management. His comfortable gut and Eddie Bauer clothes indicated he might retire in the next few years. Doris worked at a local car dealership, handling payroll part-time for spending money. She wore billowy clothes and ill-matched scarves, not to mention a perpetual gaze of spacey idealism. She drove a Volvo with one of those "practice random kindness and senseless acts of beauty" bumper stickers, if that gives you any idea.

Those probably don't seem like very charitable descriptions, do they? I promise that I don't view my clients as "suckers" or "marks" or anything exploitative like that. I'm just trained to read and interpret texts within an inch of their lives, looking for betrayals of unintended meaning. Like the Sidwells, all of us are living texts who flaunt our signs and symbols with little consciousness. The nice thing to say is that I use these signs and symbols to sell a house perfectly compatible with your dreams. The truer thing to say is that I'm looking for the obvious lever to your neuroses.

What? I'm a real estate agent, for God's sake.

Doris's first sign when she climbed down from the ostentatiously tall Austin and Prock Associates loaner Suburban was a good one: she held her hand up to her face and squeaked.

"Is there room for my studio?"

Now, see, she could have said, "Is there room for *a* studio?" But she was already thinking of it as hers, however subconsciously, which meant something right away appealed to her about the house.

Your job as a real estate agent is to keep that personal involvement going, so I replied, "There's a corner room perfect for your writing table. Plenty of room beneath the windows to cuddle up with a legal pad."

She clapped her hands together, grinning. What can I say? I like to make people happy.

Nolan drizzled from the passenger door like a dollop of cookie batter and sauntered across the lawn. He looked the house up and down, eyes squinted.

"New roof?"

"Yes, sir. Plenty of other new things, too," I replied. "Completely redecorated kitchen, brand new bathroom fixtures, and an upstairs master suite with its own Jacuzzi tub."

A woman in her twenties came jogging by on her way to the park, two greyhounds trotting by her side. Her sports bra curled tightly beneath her breasts and sweat shone on her abdomen. While Doris jiggled the door handle impatiently, Nolan took a long appreciative gaze at the jogger, watching her all the way into the park.

I unlocked the door for Doris and held it open. "Nolan?"

He turned. "Lot of young folks around here?"

"It's a mixed neighborhood, young and young-at-heart." That almost hurt to say aloud. "People exercise in the park all the time, and sometimes college kids will sun out in the field by Herschel Street."

He sidled past me through the door. Then we followed Doris and her clattering gold pumps across the hardwood floor.

"Look at the tiled fireplace surround!" she cried.

"That go all the way through to the roof?" Nolan asked.

Well, except for the body the orangutan shoved in there. "Yes, sir, all the way past the new insulation and wiring, too. It's shallow because these were coal fireplaces."

"Oh, my God!" Doris's voice echoed from the kitchen. "All new appliances!"

If you wrapped a Port-o-Let in thin stainless steel sheeting, people would push you to the ground to buy it. "Just replaced a few months ago," I said. "And those counters are granite, of course—chosen to match the tile. The cabinets are stained pine with adjustable shelves."

"Where are the knobs?" Nolan demanded, probably not for the first time in his life.

"The owner thought a buyer would want to pick those out." I swept my arm toward the dining room. "Let's step through here toward the bathroom and downstairs bedrooms, shall we?"

Touring a house is a strange ritual. Nobody quite knows what to do. They stick their heads in a room, check to make sure it is indeed a bedroom or bathroom, sometimes announcing their own plans for it: "These drapes are out of here," or "This is the perfect size for a nursery." The men always quip the women will get most of the closet.

It's tough on men, especially the kind who kick tires and open hoods to look like savvy consumers. There's not much of that to do inside a house, though some will flip open a circuit breaker to stare dumbly at the switches or peer under the sink to make sure the toilet isn't connected directly to the faucet. A few carry tape measures that they'll clatter along the floors. One or two will knock on the walls or check the ceilings. They'll nod, and you'll imagine them thinking, "Yep. Looks plumb to me."

Nolan did all of that while Doris rushed breathless from room to room like a heroine in a Gothic novel. When she trotted up the stairs, we plodded after like men with business to discuss.

"We've seen a lot of houses, Finlay," Nolan growled to me from the side of his mouth. "Always something wrong with them. The light. The smell. The neighbors. Popcorn-textured ceilings. Outdated fixtures. Whatever." We reached the second floor. "She's been dreaming about a house like this a long time, a place to retire and write her nutty book."

"What about you, Mr. Sidwell? Is this the house you've dreamed about?" People expect a little cheesiness from their real estate agent; it makes them feel they're onto you. I try to deliver.

He stared over my shoulder with an intensity that made me wonder if he was gazing at a ghost; it turns out he just wasn't looking me in the eye. "My dream house is the one we have now, only ten years ago—with the pool and the volleyball net and the kids around to use them. With Charlotte not coming home from college much, I guess we don't need all that anymore." He shook his head. "I miss the sound of her friends coming over, horsing around, having fun. Kept me young, all those girls." He looked around. "Now, I guess I just want Doris to be happy."

I took "happy" to mean "quiet," especially when he winced at her shrill voice echoing from the corner bedroom.

"This is it! This is it!" she cried.

And it sure was. Just four years ago, the windowed room in which she was standing had been slick with a bloody veneer, a man's brains speckling the walls like oatmeal tossed from a baby's bowl. Carpet now hid the stained wood floors, and new wide-slatted blinds replaced the ones the victim had broken trying to claw back to his feet.

Nolan sauntered to the corner and pried two slats open with his fingers, probably hoping the jogger had finished her lap and was coming back.

Doris framed the room with her hands. "The desk can go here, the reading chair here, the bookcase beside the window. I'll have my bulletin board of plot diagrams hanging by the door so I'll see it every time I come in to work."

When they start decorating the room, you've almost got them.

"The windows face the west so I'll see the setting sun. Those leaves make a perfect shade for the middle of the day, too."

Nolan just grunted, whether at Doris or the jogger I couldn't tell.

"The walk-in closet connects between the two bedrooms in the suite," I said.

"I can write in my slippers," she said dreamily.

Nolan let the blinds snap shut again and turned to face me. "So what's the catch, Finlay?"

"The catch?" You start by playing dumb, pretending they've got you.

"This house is the best one we've seen in six months, and it's forty grand less than its appraised value. I checked online."

The Internet makes everybody an expert, doesn't it? "Well, the appraised value is just an estimate based on comparable properties in the neighborhood and the opinion of some city employee. I mean, what is 'value,' really, but what someone is willing to pay?"

"Why isn't anybody willing to pay forty grand more for this place, then?"

Here you look away and swallow like the job is up. Then you put your hands on your hips in the "no-more-bullshit" position. I sighed, too, for a little emphasis.

"Let me be candid with you, Mr. Sidwell. This house is undervalued because some buyers are squeamish about its history."

"Its history?" Doris asked.

"I'm sure you saw online that this house was built in 1924. A lot happens in a place that old—births, fights, love, sadness." I paused. "Sometimes a murder."

Doris grimaced. Nolan narrowed his eyes.

"Now," I said, holding out my hands, "every affected surface has been replaced or thoroughly cleaned since the incident, and the house is just waiting for better memories to be made in it."

Nolan folded his arms, never a good sign. "How long ago was the…incident?"

People buying stigmatized property seem to think human pain has some kind of radioactive half-life, that there's a magical time period after which the house is "clean" again. Yeah, ask the people in Amityville.

"About four years," I replied. "There was a domestic dispute between a dentist and—"

"—his wife," Doris finished for me. "Pauline Wilmot! This is *that* house?"

Obviously Doris liked to read the crime blotter between her random acts of kindness. I checked her expression, her stance, her hands, her eyes for any signs of choosing this house on purpose. It had been the last on the list, true, but sometimes weirdoes go looking for stigmatized houses—maybe to drive a hard bargain on the price, maybe to wallow in the notoriety.

Doris was definitely a weirdo, but she looked to be an earnest one. Her surprised eyes and anxious hand-clasping seemed more like excitement over a coincidence she'd likely call "synchronicity" than glee at watching a master plan come together. But then, signs are slippery, aren't they?

"Yes, ma'am, it is," I replied.

"She killed her husband," Doris explained to Nolan. "For...being terrible."

Well, that was true enough. Doctor Wilmot sometimes administered a little more desflurane with his nitrous oxide than medically necessary, especially to younger women visiting during emergency hours for a cracked tooth or a lost filling. Some had reported odd bruises and abrasions later in places on their bodies not useful to a dentist. Pauline Wilmot, coming downstairs from the apartment to the office one evening, had caught the doctor with his final patient: their nineteen-year-old daughter, home from college to have her father pull a wisdom tooth, limply compliant in his chair.

"So it wasn't as much a murder as..." I trailed off. It *was* a murder, though maybe a useful one.

"Putting a sick dog down," Doris suggested helpfully. "She wrote all about it in her book, *A Mother's Sacrifice*."

That had been the Oprah Book Club selection Pauline had written from the state prison in Starke. I wouldn't have imagined it was a book Doris Sidwell would read, but who doesn't like a good inspirational murder story?

"She attacked him here from behind," I said to Nolan, whose brow looked more wrinkled than it had been.

Pauline had lunged forward, really, with an antique iron they'd been using as a doorstop. She swung it some ten or fifteen times into Doctor Wilmot's head, shrieking like a Valkyrie riding into battle. They found the iron lodged in his neck, she hit him so hard through the skull. Afterward, she did terrifying things to him with those instruments. I take earplugs with me to my own dentist now so I don't have to hear that little suction wand.

But these lurid details don't sell a house. You can't use words like "lunged" or "shrieked" or "suction." You've got to leave it clinical. This was an "attack" or an "incident," not a "slaying."

Doris raised her fingers to her lips. Through them, she said, "Is it haunted?"

Well, really: define "haunted." Isn't it funny how hauntings happen to the worst possible people at the worst possible times, people who are themselves struggling with more tangible horrors—divorce, death, adolescence? The Ushers certainly learned that house foundations aren't the only ones to crack. Do ghosts seek people with the same problems they have, or is it the other way around? Either way, a haunting is just the gossip of the dead intermingling with the gossip of the living, when you think about it.

Whatever the cause, I do know that Rule Number Two in the stigmatized property game is that a house is never haunted when you sell it. If the buyers choose to haunt it themselves later, that's up to them. You're selling a mirror, not a portrait.

"No one has seen any phenomena, if that's what you're asking." I shrugged. "Perhaps the Wilmots took their—"

Now I struggled for the perfect word for Doris's world view. Haunting? Neurosis? History? Spirit? Ah, there it was.

"—*karma* with them."

The Sidwells were quiet. This is Waterloo time in the sale, when you walk into another room and let your clients talk things over, when you let them sell themselves the house.

"I'll give you a moment. Take your time," I said, slipping through the door and into the other bedroom. From there, I could see the street through swaying branches of the aged live oak tree, leaves casting shadows on the Suburban, streams of Spanish moss drizzling almost to the ground. Nolan and Doris whispered together in the kill suite.

I stared at the magnetic door sign for Austin and Prock Associates, thinking about how Doris's own car was redolent with signs of its own back in the agency parking lot—*Writer's Digest* magazines on the front seat where Nolan would normally sit, notebooks scattered all over the back. You can't swing your arms in Riverside without knocking off a writer's horn-rimmed glasses, and the first work we create is ourselves.

What was Doris creating? I thought about that kooky bumper sticker, *practice random kindness and senseless acts of beauty*, and wondered over its meaning to her. "Practicing" kindness isn't the same as being kind, is it? Doesn't it imply build-up, development, faking it until making it? It really shows an ambition to be kind, a promise. A hope. With her bumper sticker, Doris seemed to be hoping for less order, less sense, more kindness, and more beauty.

And we hope for what we don't already have. Perhaps Doris sensed things she didn't want to sense any longer, and now she craved the freedom of randomness to perform her acts of beauty. As for what those acts were, a husband like Nolan and an interest in *A Mother's Sacrifice* gave me some idea.

I found myself looking forward to Doris's book. Or any of her other acts of beauty.

The Sidwells had stopped whispering. I leaned through the doorway to check on them. They were standing in separate corners, Doris looking right at me and Nolan watching the street with his hands rattling change in the pockets of his chinos.

I approached, arms folded behind my back. "What are you thinking?" I asked quietly.

Doris shook her head. "Nolan likes it, especially the park. There's room for Charlotte to come home for Christmas with her friends, if she wants." She sighed. "But I don't know for sure. Do you think it would affect my writing? Things like that don't just go away."

I nodded. "Well, I'm not sure what Pauline was thinking on the day she killed her husband." I said "killed" somewhat sharply. "She could well have been a woman of deep passions, probably long held close, smothered after years of forced silence. Something about this room focused those passions, certainly."

Doris lowered her hand from her mouth.

"It's easy for us to think it was a crime with the little we know," I said. "Justice has a way of taking care of itself, especially with the help of sensitive people. Crime or not, Pauline followed her heart despite all the consequences." I shrugged. "Maybe for the first time."

Rule Number Three for selling stigmatized property? You don't ignore the stigma; you match it to the right person. I think Emily Dickinson wrote that "one need not be a chamber to be haunted," and I've learned that you sell haunted houses to haunted people. There's sure no shortage of either.

"We'll take it," she said.

She Shells

She'd been down there for days, her long brown hair washing back and forth with the tide.

The best the men could tell, she'd somehow gotten lodged in the colony of mussels clinging to the seawall, and repeated proddings with long poles and hooks hadn't managed to get her free. The current was swift and more often than not, the best you'd do was jab her in the face. If you got the hook around her neck, the head would seem to slither out of it. Tommy and Harold got a rope around her waist, but they couldn't pull her free even with six more of us pulling along behind them. Even connected to the front bumper of Garrett's Ford, that rope preferred to fray and give way rather than get her loose.

Oxwell the coroner was for just letting the body break off naturally in a few days on account of nobody coming out to claim her, but that didn't seem right. Maybe she had kin up the river a few miles. They'd be sure to wonder where she was, and when they came down to ask us, it might be nice to have something more than a story to give them.

So we got Frank outfitted in his diving gear and sent him down to see what was what. Usually, Frank did repairs to our boats and piers in the good season, and he was the best in the business. A real no-nonsense guy: go down, get it done, come back.

We set him up a ladder and compressor rig while he put on the thick gray suit and its heavy brass helmet. We helped him tighten the screws until his breath fogged the little circle of glass, and he gave us the thumbs up as he climbed down the ladder.

We had some limited communication from him through the hose apparatus, and his breathing was calm and constant all the way down into the water. He called off six feet and then twelve feet, and then he got real quiet.

It was almost a minute before he spoke. "She's in here real good," he said. "These shells are almost up to her waist."

"You be careful down there!" Tommy shouted, as though his voice would have to carry through the water. "Those will cut you right up."

The next thing we heard after several grunts of effort was a whisper. "What the hell is that?"

"What is what?" Tommy said, and we all leaned over the seawall to see what we could see. The body was still gently swaying in the current, and the hair was caressing his helmet.

"Jesus," Frank said next. "Jesus Christ."

We watched him helplessly as he reached for the ladder. He'd gotten one hand and one foot on it before something pulled him back. We could feel the solid thunk of his helmet against the concrete through our feet, and the dark cloud blooming was unmistakable.

"Pull him up! Pull him up!" Tommy was drawing the hose up hand over hand when something pulled back against it. The hose whipped to one side and then the other, nearly knocking all of us in. It then pulled completely taut as though it held onto something impossibly heavy.

"Pull, God damn you!" cried Tommy, but we couldn't even get our fingers underneath it.

We heard another sickening clunk and then the low scrape of metal, and then the line fell slack. It was nothing at all to pull the hose then—it all but flew through our hands—and the wrinkled knot of brass that was once Frank's helmet just landed at our feet like the discarded core of an apple. Blood still trickled from where the neck had been, and nobody wanted to guess how much of the head was still inside.

The ladder shook next, finally falling away from the dock in one last message: don't come down here again.

And we haven't. Even though she's still there. Even though the other shells have sprouted her little sisters, a dozen or more, with their tiny tufts of greasy raven hair and little white arms reaching, reaching, reaching upwards toward us.

Prudenter to Dream

By the time the raccoon dropped from the tree and landed belly-deep in the middle of her birthday cake, Missy Irving was done with her party. Her idiot brother and his idiot friends had been chasing the girls around the picnic tables with handfuls of dog poop, and the adults were too busy smoking and laughing together to do anything about it. Really, the raccoon was a perfect distraction; while everybody jumped up to chase it away, she could finally make her escape.

Mom would probably be mad at her for being rude, slinking away like that, but she was having the headache again and her book was a lot more quiet than any of those kids. And besides, she was nine now and too old for birthday parties.

So Missy slipped away under the tree shadows, carrying her book in one hand and a slice of un-raccooned birthday cake in the other, in case she needed rations.

She found the farthest picnic table in Boone Park, one near the tree line beneath a drooping old live oak. Beards of Spanish moss almost reached the table, so it was perfectly cool and shaded and hidden. She sat down, opened her book, and propped her head in her hands to read.

That's when the man in the gray suit stepped from behind the tree.

"Ah," he said, and she jumped. "So this is where you've been hiding."

For like two whole minutes, thought Missy. She reached for her book and her cake, ready to be frog-marched back to the party like an escaped convict, but then she realized that none of the adults there had been wearing a suit. He was a stranger, standing out in the wet grass behind the trees by himself, maybe even waiting for her.

When Missy glanced back toward the party, it seemed a long way away. "My mom is right over there."

The man nodded. "Very good thinking, not talking to strangers. Very *secure* thinking. I completely approve. But then, I'm not a stranger to you, Melissa Irving."

He knew her name. He was a stranger who knew her name.

The man leaned closer, hands in his pants pockets with the suit jacket scrunched up over them. "Don't you recognize me?"

Missy looked him over. He seemed ordinary, maybe a little taller and thinner than most, and he was wearing an ordinary suit with a gray jacket and gray pants and a thin blue tie. The tie was loose and the collar open, like Daddy sometimes looked when he came home late from work.

He leaned even closer. "Not at all? Not a little bit?"

"No," she said.

The man sighed. "Well, that's to be expected, given everything." He nodded toward the kids yelling on the other side of the park. "That your birthday party?"

Missy couldn't think of any harm in saying that it was, so she nodded.

"How old are you today?"

She didn't see much harm in confessing that, either. "I'm nine."

"Nine." He looked to one side and then the other before taking a step closer. "That's a good age, nine. If I could, I'd be nine again, too. What made you choose nine?"

"I didn't choose it. Nine was the next number after eight."

"Ah," the man said. "But what if you did choose it? What if I told you that, say, you were only dreaming that you were nine? That you're really, oh, let's call it forty-six years old?"

She squinted at him. That couldn't be right. She didn't remember going to bed, she didn't remember being married or having a job. But then, the harder she thought about it, the less she remembered about her day at the park, either.

"What are you talking about? Who are you?"

"Well, ma'am, I'm a friend. Which is good, because you need one now more than ever. I'm Avram Weyrich, the White House Chief of Staff."

Missy frowned. "What are you doing here?"

The man sat down beside her, and though she considered sidling away, she didn't. She wasn't sure why.

"I'm here because you're here, but 'here' isn't where you think it is. Right now, you're lying unconscious in the intensive care unit of the base hospital at Jacksonville

Naval Air Station. You've been wounded in the deadliest assassination in American history."

"Me?"

"You were traveling with the President from a fund-raising dinner when terrorists attacked the motorcade with three suicide car bombers and a Cessna 210, flown under radar from a little airport in Keystone Heights. Loaded with a quarter ton of C-4."

"Oh, my God," she said. "Is the President okay?"

"I'm sorry to say, ma'am, that he's not. He died on impact. Worse still, the Vice-President passed away six weeks ago from a stroke and a replacement has yet to be appointed. The next in the line of Presidential succession is the Speaker of the House." He pointed. "You are the Speaker of the House."

Missy felt dizzy for a moment, thinking that over. "Am I okay?"

"You're comatose. We're communicating with you through this big tangle of wires flashing images in your brain."

Speaker of the House. That sounded like a big job. "What do I do all day?"

"You're presiding officer of the House of Representatives. You help the President set the legislative agenda. You represent the Florida fourth congressional district. You're also the ranking member of the House Committee on Foreign Affairs, with your specialty being matters of peacekeeping and counterterrorism."

"That sounds boring."

He shook his head. "Not today."

"You're just teasing, right? You're just the smartest crazy bum who ever lived or something, and you're playing a joke on me."

"Oh, I wish I were, I really do. I can see why you'd rather be here, believe me." The man patted her hand. "The doctors say it's a retreat to a happier state, a common psychological defense."

"Are the bad guys still trying to hurt me?"

"No, you're safe. We've locked down the Jacksonville airspace, closed I-95 at both junctions to I-295, blocked all state and county roads into the city, and nationalized the Florida and Georgia Guard. Every person in this hospital has sworn to protect the United States, and right now—you're the United States."

Missy glanced back toward the party and saw her mother standing beside one of the tables, cigarette dangling from her mouth, arms full of torn wrapping paper. She seemed to be looking around, probably for her.

"That's my mom," Missy said to the man. "She won't like me talking to you."

"It can't be helped. We're running out of time. The President pro tempore is next in line after you, and he's from a party that...well, doesn't share our commitment to security. Agents are on their way to the Colorado wilderness to find him on his hunting trip, but in the meantime, you're in command of the armed forces of the United States. We're in a state of war and only you can make the very big decision America needs."

"What kind of decision?"

"We need to demonstrate to our enemies and allies that we're still strong and not struggling in confusion or fear. The markets open in fourteen hours, and the Fed chairman says there will be a two-thousand point drop in the Dow unless someone demonstrates that America is still open for business."

"What business?"

"The business of preserving liberty for all the world. The U.S.S. Ronald Reagan carrier group has entered the Persian Gulf, and the submarine U.S.S. Ohio has Trident III nuclear-capable missiles aimed at Tehran and two major military bases known to harbor terrorist trainees and high-ranking Iranian intelligence officers. Signal intercepts this morning from their defense ministry indicated foreknowledge of the attack and the possibility of more."

That couldn't be good. "What am I supposed to do?"

The man squeezed her hand. "All we need from you is a go code."

"What's a go code?"

"It's like a key. Or a password. It would give us permission to proceed, to launch the missile attack."

"Will people die?"

The man paused, seeming to listen. All Missy heard was the drone of locusts from behind him in the bushes. "They're estimating in the Situation Room that 20,000 could die in an attack on the capital."

Missy's stomach twisted like a dish rag when Mom squeezed the water out. "That's a lot of people."

"We call it a 'proportional response.'"

Missy wasn't sure what that meant. "Would I do it if I was awake?" She motioned behind him. "Where I'm an adult?"

The man smiled with his lips thin and tight. "Well, you've written fifty papers on peacekeeping. You're one of the most widely-traveled Representatives in history, visiting dangerous places all over the world. You were quite likely to be appointed Secretary of State during the President's second term. You know the uses of peace." His voice got low. "And you know the uses of war."

"I don't know anything."

"Somewhere you do. The world's becoming a Nostradamus quatrain out here: the PRC is firing test missiles in the Taiwan Strait, troops are mobilizing in the Sudan, and the Russians are already flying sorties over Iran. We've got messages from Moscow and Beijing asking what our stance is going to be, and I know you'll agree with me when I say that our stance should be don't fuck with the eagle, if you don't mind my saying."

"You just said the f-word."

"Yes, I did. And were you not nine years old, you'd probably agree that this is the perfect time to say the f-word. Say it with me."

She scrunched her nose.

"Come on. It'll do you good. Just once. 'Fuck.'"

Well, nobody would hear, and she always wanted to try it. "Fuck," she mumbled.

"Come on." The man tapped his chest. "Convince me."

"Fuck!" Missy cried. It felt good. No wonder her parents said it all the time.

"Great. Now say 'sons of bitches.'"

She looked at him aghast. One swear a day was all she could handle, along with being the Speaker of the House. "Do I even like you? I mean, back there?"

He laughed with his mouth but not with his eyes. "What a thing to ask. Of course you like me. We're colleagues, working toward liberty at home and across the globe. We don't always agree at first, but you usually come around to my way of thinking, one way or another. At least the President does."

"I don't want to do it," she said. "It's dumb. It won't work. When we kick the boys back for chasing us, it just makes us chase them more."

He closed his eyes. "Madam Speaker, we're not in a playground out here. A bunch of psychology and policy wonks are trying to figure out what the metaphor is. The going theory is that the kid in the Harry Potter hat somehow represents the Ayatollah, but that doesn't do us much good."

"That's my brother. He started it."

"I'm sure." He put both his hands on her shoulders. "But the focus here and now is on protecting the country. And the only way you can do that—the *only* way—is to launch those missiles."

"But if I do, won't I be as bad?"

"Well, that's the silver lining to this thing, Madam Speaker. In a few hours, another person will be sworn in as President of the United States. Anything we do in the meantime was ordered by a chief executive who is, to put it kindly, a little out of the jurisdiction of international law. That's your ticket to do the necessary things America can't normally consider."

"But won't I get in trouble when I wake up?"

"Madam Speaker, there's a very good chance you're not *going* to wake up. You're asleep, hiding in the memories of a nine-year-old kid. Your body is a mangled husk, your liver and kidneys are failing, your every breath is supplied by the grace of a ventilator. To be blunt, Madam Speaker, you're a brain in a jar at this point."

That had to be horrible, laying there on a table with a bunch of people in uniforms running all around, wires sticking out of her, generals and admirals fighting over everything she thought. That was only now. After that, she'd be alone.

"Aw, come on," said the man. "It isn't all that bad. I was being a little hyperbolic, that's all. I mean, it's good, isn't it, that you get to spend this time again with your friends and family? You've earned it. All we need is the go code—"

"And I kill all those people?"

"Of course not, honey. The *missiles* kill all those people. Missiles you don't have to see or hear about. Missiles preserving the safety of our great nation."

"Why don't you just say I said 'go'?"

The man laughed hollowly, looking around. "Well, that would be unethical, wouldn't it? Your position demands a certain respect—"

"Then don't do it. Do something else."

The man threw up his hands. "There is no 'something else.' We have to make a show of strength, demonstrate that we're not caught on our heels. We can't let them get away with it."

Missy looked back toward her birthday party, now lapsed into chaos. Alexis swung a branch at Dylan, and Heather kicked at one of the mothers from the top of the table. Inside it all, she could see her mother grab Marcus by the collar and drag him away from a weeping cousin, a pine cone still clutched in his hand. Missy's mom steered him toward a tree and parked him at the base. His Harry Potter hat was gone.

Of all the places to come to in a dream, why here? Why this stupid birthday party with her stupid brother and his stupid friends? Missy watched Mom lecture Marcus awhile. Then she thought of something.

"You know," she said to the man, "when we act up, Mom puts us in Time Out. Can't you do that?"

"Mom isn't defending democracy from the raging hordes of unreason."

"She just takes me by the arm or him by the arm and puts us in our room."

He shook his head. "So does that mean a Special Forces intervention? Is that what you're suggesting? Just capturing these guys?"

"Mom doesn't have to burn our house down to show she's in charge."

The man in the suit got quiet. Then, he spoke again, slowly. "Well, that's an excellent point, Madam Speaker, one we're happy to weigh in all due course. Of course, we'd need a go code to confirm that you're competent to give the order—"

"I'm competent!" she cried.

"Well, without the codes…"

She couldn't remember any codes.

The man in the suit watched her. "Anything?" he asked. "Any words coming to you, strange ones? Foxtrot? Alpha? Niner? Anything like that?"

She closed her eyes and thought real hard but she couldn't think of any funny words.

"Just say whatever comes to mind. Anything at all. Numbers, letters, animal names."

"Hey!" A shout came behind them.

They both jumped and turned. Missy was glad to see her mother had come.

"What the hell are you doing with my daughter?"

"I'm briefing her, ma'am, and you'd do best to stand clear."

"'Briefing' her?" Mom rushed forward and pulled Missy off the picnic table by her arm. "That's a new one."

"He's the White House Chief of Staff," Missy explained, in case it helped.

"Oh, yeah?" Mom pointed. "What's your name, 'Chief'?"

The man held up a hand. "You wouldn't recognize it, I'm sure."

"Really?" She jabbed a finger over his shoulder. "You think the cops would recognize a child molester?"

He craned his neck around her. "Anything, Madam Speaker?" He smiled in a tight, creepy way. "Madam President? A number, a book, a person's name."

Missy clenched her eyes closed. In the flashes she saw behind her eyelids, she saw—A snake? A train? She wasn't sure, but something made her say, "Boxcar."

The man's eyes widened. "Yes? Anything else?"

Missy got a sick feeling in her stomach looking at that smile; it wasn't the smile of a guy who wanted to be good, that she knew. So, too, did her mother, who stepped forward and pushed her hand against the man's chest.

"That's *all* you're getting," Mom said.

The man looked around quickly, stumbling back. "Madam Speaker, millions of people are counting on you."

"Well, they'll have to count on somebody else, buddy." Mom was walking faster now, and the man was trying to keep up as he retreated. "And you can count on me calling the cops if I ever see you here again."

He held up his hands, trying to smile. "Look, I—"

"Beat it!" Mom shoved him and he fell back into the muck with a satisfying *squish*. Too stunned to do anything else, he stared up at them as he sank a few inches. Missy watched her mother's hands tighten into fists, and she wondered if Mom would hit him even while he was down. She kind of hoped so.

Slowly, the man flailed back to his feet, leaving behind an imprint in the mud that looked like a gingerbread man. "You've failed America, Madam Speaker," he said.

Mom flipped him the bird and held it, driving him off with its power until he limped off to the woods. As they watched him disappear into the thick undergrowth, Missy leaned close to her mother. Nine was the best one to choose, the best party, the best time when Mom could still scare trouble away.

Now she always would.

Illustration by Elizabeth Shippen Green

Mom in the Misted Lands

The good news? Mom was out of bed. The bad news? She was blocking the way to the tree house while wearing her sheet as a dress.

"Uh, Mom?" Rick asked.

"Yes, Ricardo, son of the Bastard?" Mrs. Dominguez said, her fingers tracing the bark of the oak tree in front of their house. Her feet, bare, wedged one atop the other in the notch that Rick and the guys used to climb up into their fort.

"Yeah," he replied, glancing at his buddies. Herb stared at his own Keds. Walter shifted the baseball bat out from under one arm to the other. Paulie squinted at Rick's mother as though she was the noontime sun.

"You, uh, mind if we climb up real quick for our baseball stuff? Chip and some older kids got a scratch game going behind Mr. Bowen's grocery."

"Baseball," she breathed. "Hardly the sport of the Queen's men."

Rick blotted sweat off the back of his neck. Jesus, this was embarrassing.

"I don't guess so," he said finally. "But, you know, they're waiting on us and—"

"Blunt clubs and leather mittens are the toys of *children*," Mom said. The safety pin holding the sheet together over her right olive-hued shoulder gave way, letting the improvised sleeve slip down her arm. "I need *men* to ride with me into Thuria."

Rick, twelve, had never heard of Thuria, but he wondered if Coach Simmons would be talking about it next Fall in Health class. He wondered, too, if maybe he ought to help his mother back into the house and get her some water or something. Call Doctor Hargis, maybe.

"The Misted Lands?" she said, letting herself swing dangerously far from the tree by only one hand. "The Groves of Succor? The Sacred Fountains of Urlog? All blackened with the creeping smut of the dread Lord Mung? Peopled with the once proud citizens of Thuria, now cowering slaves?"

Walter held his hand up to his brow to shade out the sun. "You know, Mrs. Dominguez, the hatch is, like, two feet over your head. If you could just reach and—"

"You'll all need blades, of course. Broadswords for Herbert and Paul to suit your arms, rapiers for Walter and Richard. Leather jerkins, too. Gauntlets of hardened boar hide. Higher boots for navigating the Stinging Marshes." She peered above their heads, somewhere down Jasper Lane.

"The journey will be hard, that's all I can promise, but the cause is just."

"Forget it," Rick said, turning. He motioned the guys back. "We'll use Chip's old bat instead."

"Wait!" Mom cried. She braced herself to the tree with one slender leg, unshaven from three weeks in bed. The hair on it was black. "Do you deny a woman in need for vengeance? He rode away in the night, you know, off with his harlot, the oh-very-brave Charlotte, the oh-very-honorable Charlotte."

Rick hadn't met Charlotte yet, but Dad was living in her apartment across from the University as far as he knew. Sometimes he'd ridden his bike from his father's office to his classroom and then back through the potholed streets of what they called the student ghetto. He'd stared up at drooping air conditioner units, at faded posters of Jimi Hendrix, at plain white sheets snapping in the breeze—wondering which one his father lived behind now.

"Come on, Mom, I'll help you home," Rick said, holding out his hand.

Mom recoiled back into the tree. "Home? My home is Thuria. My home is the rampart of Castle Jasper, calling the men to arms."

"Mom," Rick said again, this time risking a touch upon her calf. It was cold and sticky like an ice tray.

"I'm epic, too," she said, too quietly for anyone but Rick to hear. He wasn't sure what she meant, but the only things Dad had taken from their house were the books full of legends and journeys.

There wasn't anything to do, Rick thought—nothing dignified, anyway. She was perched in that tree but good, and it would take all four of them to get her down, likely screaming and cursing the whole way. Mrs. Pettyjohn next door would come out in her housecoat to scowl. Someone would call the fire department or the cops. Someone else might splash her quickly with the hose to "snap her out of it."

She already was out of it.

Rick swallowed. There wasn't much to try but let her do...whatever she was doing. To burn itself out, like Grandpa's binges. She wasn't far off the ground; she couldn't hurt herself. She was fifty feet from the door.

"I think we'll get going now, Mom," Rick said. "Sorry to bother you. When I get home, I'll make dinner." Again. Rick had been boiling cans of stew for weeks ever since Dad left and Mom took to bed with her books.

"Will none of you join me?" she cried. "Will none of you stand for justice?"

Paulie stepped forward, clutching his Rays cap in his fists. "I will, Mrs. Dominguez. I'll stand for justice. I'll go to the Misted Lands."

Rick shot him a glare. That wouldn't help, Paulie encouraging her. Paulie with his comic books. Paulie with his secret treasure maps. Paulie with his *Dungeons & Dragons*. Paulie with his ghost stories, his army men, his plastic bucket helmet. Paulie who was growing up way slower than the rest of them, taking his time.

Paulie he'd left behind, but with the empty sensation that maybe Paulie was leaving him behind.

"Let us ride, then, you and I," Mom said. Taking Paulie's hand, she descended from the tree like a lady stepping down from a carriage. She didn't let go and neither did Paulie.

"She's my mom," Rick hissed.

"Whither hence, Mrs. Dominguez?" Paulie said in his weird way.

"Quickly, to the gates!"

Together, hand in hand, not looking back, they ran between Rick's house and Mrs. Pettyjohn's. They ducked beneath the drooping willow in the back, vaulted over the fence, and disappeared somewhere behind the deep brush of the woods.

Rick didn't move for a long time. He watched and waited until Herb and Walter had each gone home to their own mother's calls. He stood there as the sun descended, holding his baseball glove.

Finally, he went inside and made himself some stew.

The Ghost Factory

Worthington Wood isn't a forest but a hospital—a sprawling and defunct mental facility crumbling into the primeval Florida landscape like the ruins of Tikal. Built during the Second World War as a training airfield, the Wood sits thirty miles from civilization amid yellowed grass, low oak trees sagging under Spanish moss, spindly pines, and knots of leathery palmetto. Its dozen concrete block buildings sit baking in the heat, their state-sanctioned pastel colors fading to a sickening hue of governmental decay.

People still live here, people you can't quite see. People no one ever quite saw. I guess you'd call them ghosts, and they were my patients.

Now I'm theirs.

The first thing to know about me is that I'm the worst case worker in the history of the Wood, and that's really saying something for a state institution. I mean, I took my first college course in psychology because I was curious how other people learned to feel when I hadn't, and I stuck around in the program because it was still a little sexy in 1975 to pretend I was helping the world. Over the gentle gurgle of a beer can bong, I could say things like, "If we could perfect the science of empathy, man, we could totally stop our planet's death trip," and it would get me into some girl's dorm bed.

Thirty-odd years and two divorces later, I still haven't perfected the science of empathy. Counseling is a vocation for listeners in a society of talkers, and the only reason I had a career at all is that my ambivalence closely resembled listening. I didn't "advise" my clients like all my colleagues did, and I let the screwballs carry the conversation while I thought about other things—whether it was worth going back to school to study computers, maybe, or if anybody like me could get away with a heist like D.B. Cooper's.

Crazy people are a lot less interesting than you'd expect. For one thing, they're literally hard to understand: they ramble in long torrents of learned psychological jargon, sometimes with random realizations that the rest of us take for granted. You know that feeling you got when you realized that every tiny star was a sun? They get it for things like figuring out that all the doors on the ward open outward or that it's possible to eat cake with a spoon. They're addicted to epiphany, a little like drunks—drunks who sit on the couch in your office and pick their toes or hold their fingers in their mouths. Most of them are fixated on some terrible event or wound or misconception, chasing theories off a cliff. Pretty much like all of us.

Not long after I started here, I saw a guy argue with a tree. He was this huge turtle of a man, bare flesh hanging down his back, yelling at a pine, pointing in all directions and shaking his fist while the tree took it all with aplomb.

I watched between my office blinds as things escalated. First there was a shove. Then, a bump of the chest. Finally, the guy leaned back, wound up his arm like Roger Clemens, and socked that tree but good at full force.

The man grabbed his arm, hopping and swearing. I could have intervened. I could have broken up the argument. I could have, you know, called someone over from the Infirmary at least. But I let those blinds snap into place again because I didn't want to do the paperwork.

I know, I know: it makes me sick, too.

In one of my final reviews before we shut down for good, Doctor Federovich asked me straight out, "Do you even give a shit about these people?"

I sat there blinking, wondering how to answer. "Well, sir," I said finally, "I don't think they want my shit."

We're surrounded here at the Wood by a pasture on one side, a lonely state highway on another, and a thick swampy forest on the other two. It's not just any kind of forest, either: it's Florida forest, all Jurassic-looking with chest-high palmetto fronds and towering pines and little clearings of primordial loam, wet and sticky. It drones with locusts all day and all night, the sound of nascent life straining to evolve.

They've long since cut the power, so it's dark enough to see the stars at night—even the Milky Way. I sit on the porch of one of the old doctor's cottages, waiting and watching.

Every few nights when I'm tired or drunk, I'll see them pass, my old patients. I can't *want* to see them, I can't try: they somehow know when you aren't quite looking. It's only from the blurred edges of my vision that I see the train of hospital gowns winding in silence between the buildings, hand linked to hand, maybe a hundred of them. They cross the scrabbly lawn, making gentle sounds, whispering and giggling from one end to the other like a pulse down a single giant neuron. When they get to the edge of the fence going out or coming back, they pass through without even pausing.

Valerie is always last, and sometimes she turns to look at me before she's through. She hasn't beckoned, though, so I haven't followed.

Valerie came to Worthington Wood in 1990. The money for her care came from her father, an attorney in a nearby town who didn't need a nutty daughter wandering around to ruin a good thing. She was the only resident of the Wood to arrive with matching luggage, two powder blue suitcases packed with heels, skirts, blouses, slacks, t-shirts, underwear, hose, scarves, and books (I remember *The Grapes of Wrath*, *Heart of Darkness*, and *Helter Skelter*, but there were more). Oh, and a make-up case with a mirror on the inside of the lid.

When she wasn't sunning in her Wayfarers on the smoking patio, she passed from counselor to counselor. She started with Pauline, a specialist in art therapy who encouraged her to paint or sculpt, and the result was a striking series of realistic crime scene portraits, the victims drawn as stark white silhouettes. She went on to David, whose focus on cognitive behavioral therapy provided her with a deck of index cards with practical daily advice like, "When you're angry, breathe!" In talk therapy with Beryl, Valerie recounted the plot of "A Good Man is Hard to Find" as an incident from her childhood.

When she ended up in my dark, cramped office with twenty layers of government latex paint on the walls, the first thing I asked her was, "So you came here to play with us?"

"No," she said, kicking off her shoes and folding her legs beneath her on my fraying green couch, commandeered by the state from someone's yard sale. "I came here to find out if any of you were real."

"Huh," I said. "Aren't you going to be disappointed."

She didn't say anything else and I didn't either. For that whole first session, I leaned back in my chair and doodled a spreading vine pattern across my legal pad. That's what we did for the second and third sessions, too: sat in silence.

"Is this your way of wearing me down?" she asked at the beginning of the fourth.

"No. This is my way of getting a peaceful hour in the middle of the morning," I said. "You're the quietest wacko we have." I held up one of my worn Philip K. Dick paperbacks. "You mind?"

"Be my guest," she said.

I'd made it halfway through the book two sessions later before she started talking. If I looked up, she'd stop. Like the figures I see making for the fence some nights, she didn't bear direct observation.

~

There's no electricity or running water at the Wood these days. That's less inconvenient than it sounds because I've got all the fuel I need for my lantern from the old heating oil tanks, and I collect rain water in barrels. It's fresher than the stuff on the ground or out of the old irrigation well, anyway.

What little I eat comes from a grocería about ten miles down Highway 31, a place where the migrants buy their food. A bag of corn tortillas and a couple dented cans of beans can last me weeks because, well, I'm not that hungry. I haven't been for years.

Valerie had left her withering cow town not long after high school to start college at NYU on a math scholarship. She "hit a wall," she said, in a class called Philosophy of Mathematics—no amount of study or thought could get her past it. She tried to switch to Statistics but that was worse. "Too practical," she said. "And scary to find out that everything's approximate…including me."

She'd dropped out and headed west for no other reason than she'd never been there, and she'd tried starting school again in Utah and Arizona. Somewhere in there she visited New Orleans and Mexico City, Toronto and San Diego. She tried singing in a band, modeling for art classes, even working in an Alaskan fishery for about four hours. She stayed with friends—even if she had to make them.

"I bought us all food with my dad's Shell card," she said. "You'd be surprised how long people will let you crash at their place if you're buying all the beer and snack cakes."

She saw things, she said, strange things. The LSD wasn't helping and neither was the heroin, but she'd been getting the sense that the world was getting too bright to look at quite directly. Some people glowed and others faded; she couldn't tell the difference why.

All she knew is that she was one of the faders and it scared her.

There wasn't much in her story to differentiate her from any other twenty-something with a brain, figuring out that the "system" is a sham and trying to decide if she wanted to play along. That's not a sign of being mentally ill unless you make the inconvenient choice.

When her father bought her a flight and ordered her home one Christmas, she made that choice. "I went off the rails a little," was how she put it.

A boy wasn't exactly at the center of it, but he hadn't helped. She'd been best friends with Ben in high school, talking almost every night on the phone through their junior and senior years, though they hadn't spent much time together in person outside of school.

"It was platonic as far as we knew," she said. "But come on. You can't talk about all that stuff—what you want to be when you grow up, what you think the world should be like, which teacher is sleeping with what student, how many years we have until the world breaks us down and makes us normal, all the important stuff—without being more deeply in love than anybody can be past the age of seventeen. Right?"

I knew she didn't need an answer.

"There was kind of a weird intimacy there, as though we'd skipped over that terrible awkward part of a relationship where you're fumbling your hands together and trying to figure out what to say to be romantic. I think we were too afraid that hanging out together in the real world would ruin things."

I nodded slightly, but she didn't notice.

"Anyway, I came back from the West Coast all out of my head. I can't remember if I was drinking then or not, but I sure as hell was shooting up. There's a picture of me standing by the Christmas tree with my younger sister Emma in our church dresses, and my eyes are all sunken and my hair is all crackly. I'm blurry, underexposed. I look like Nancy Spungen after a bad weekend bender, and Emma looks like Holly Hobby.

"And Ben came back from school, too. Actually, he'd finished and was getting ready to go to law school. God, law school! Not that he told me or anything: I heard from my mom who knew his mom. He was home for the summer, working for his dad's gas business. I knew it would get back to him that I was home, so I gave him a whole week to call. Of course he didn't, so I thought it'd be funny to go get his ass out of bed in the middle of the night. Your sense of humor changes when you're high, I guess."

It was hard not to wince sympathetically at that.

She shook her head. "All those years I'd known him and I'd never been to his house. They had this crazy fence like ten feet high and I almost killed myself climbing over, cutting my hands and legs to ribbons. I don't think I had shoes. I had no idea which room was his, so I ran around his yard all bloody, pressing my hands against the windows, standing on tip-toe to see inside. His parents were out of town; there were sweet little mystery novels on their nightstands. I saw his sister's room, scattered with all her cheerleading crap; she wasn't home, either. And then I came to his room. It had a set of golf clubs leaning inside the window."

I glanced up from my book, and she sat up now, no longer resting her weight on her legs. It's good to notice these things in case a client isn't ready to admit a feeling yet. Or if she's going to leap at you.

"Golf clubs. Like a good plutocrat ought to have, right? I cupped my hands to the glass and there he was, asleep. So I smack my hands against the glass a couple of times, smearing blood all over.

"He finally opens the window and says, 'Valerie! What are you doing here?' Then he says, 'What the hell happened to you? Are you okay?' And all I can say is, 'Golf clubs!' And all he says is, 'What are you talking about? Calm down, will you?' And that's when I realize he's all clean cut and confident, which is to say stupid, and I want to hurt him. I grab for the front of his pajamas—he was wearing pajamas, for Christ's sake—but he smacks my hands away and says, 'What's wrong with you?'"

She'd slid off the couch now and knelt on the floor.

"And God, I couldn't say. I couldn't talk at all, I don't think. I kind of howled. They called the cops and I ran off into his parents' orange groves."

Even in Florida, it gets chilly in the winter. I wondered how long she'd hidden in the groves, bleeding, shivering. Or maybe she didn't feel any of that at all. She didn't say.

"You know what made me mad, don't you?"

Yes, I thought I did. But she didn't want my answer.

"It was that he'd gotten his life together first. Before I did. Before asking me or taking me along. Isn't that terrible?"

I didn't break our pact to answer.

"He wasn't fucked up anymore, not like I was. I wanted to fuck him up. And I did."

You know that Valerie and I slept together, right? There's a reason she stands out among all the patients I neglected, and not just because she was the one who'd gone crazy for a more interesting reason than most.

Some guys in my position would point out that it was voluntary, which it was, and that we needed each other, which we did. But come on: I fell in love with her story, and she fell in love with my willingness to hear it.

I'm a terrible counselor, but Valerie was the first and last patient with whom I had what most people would call an "affair," though the word implies a desperate passion that wasn't there. We talked and kissed and finally made love out in one of these doctor's cottages, not like teenagers or college students but more like a tired middle-aged couple. It was slow and gentle, quiet, as though neither of us expected much.

I don't live in the same cottage we used. It was abandoned then and it's abandoned now. Built for young doctors whose families hadn't yet made the move to Florida, all these cottages have a threadbare plaid couch and twin beds, plus a chrome-edged kitchenette table in a mustard-yellow galley kitchen. The closest my cottage comes now to being haunted is my memory of how Valerie used to stand behind a similar counter in only her t-shirt, opening cabinets in search of cups for water. Those could have been quiet Sunday mornings in 1970, judging by the décor.

My cottage is two doors down. It's not haunted, not like the rest of the place. The light here comes from my lantern, and the doors lock and unlock because I latch them. The glowing windows on the ward or the doors that slam—that has nothing to do with me. Not directly.

Valerie didn't finish her story in the next session or the one after that. She looked through all my books during one hour, opening the three-ring binder manuals the state gives you for diagnosing people, maybe paging through to find herself. I hadn't decided on a diagnosis; I hadn't even thought about it. "Wacked" was about the extent, but then, that's all of us, and the doctors can't write prescriptions for "wacked."

About a week later, she told me the rest.

"I didn't go home that night," she started suddenly. "I walked all the way back to town first, hiking down Highway 70. There's this place we used to go when we were kids, an oak tree leaning out over the river with a rope hanging from a limb. It's so painfully Mayberry. You swing out onto that rope into the brown water, and you hope like hell the splash scares the alligators and moccasins away. The water is full of tannin from rotting leaves so you can't see the bottom until you're in it, either, and sometimes you knock your legs against a concrete block or an old stump down there. There are big patches of oil on the surface from the boat ramp fifty feet up the river, too. You come out looking like a bass."

I knew the kind of place.

"So that's where I went that night. I mean, the Moon was out and the air was clear, so I thought, 'Screw it, I'm going swimming.' Maybe it was one last challenge to Ben: if he knew me enough to find me there, maybe there was hope, right?"

I supposed there might be.

"And damn if he didn't find me there like three hours later. He'd gotten dressed when I ran off, tried looking for me in the groves awhile, and then drove into town in his father's Lexus. Thank God I didn't see him in it or I'd never have let him close to me. As it was, I didn't know he had the car until after.

"I'm diving under the water over and over again, pacing across the narrow point of the river there, my hair stretched flat along my back and the water flowing past my face, probably the cleanest I'd been in a month. I see the headlights flash through the trees, and a few minutes later, he's squatting atop one of the big roots you use as a step to get onto the tree, waving at me to come closer. I don't, though: I keep treading water, leaning back a little so he can see me. Can see what I wasn't wearing."

She did it then on the couch, holding out her arms like wings and closing her eyes.

"And then I start talking, everything coming out in a rush. Everything I've seen, become. Everything I am now, without him around to listen anymore." Eyes still closed, she floated her arms above the back of the couch. "The water keeps washing in and out of my ears and I'm only catching a few of my own words. I know one of them is 'alone.' Another is 'afraid.' Still another is 'lost.' I try to tell him how I don't feel like me anymore, that maybe there isn't a 'me' at all."

She rested her arms now and opened her eyes.

"I drift in closer to the shore and lift my head above the water. He's been talking, too, and I can hear now that he's been telling me about settling down, choosing a path, respecting myself, growing up, all that intervention crap. He hasn't heard anything I've said. I feel sick and cold. Soon I'm underneath that oak and I kick my leg and my leg goes right through it. Like I'm a ghost. Like I don't exist."

The water at night, I thought. Hard to tell distances, easy for the moonlight to be bent—

She glowered at me, knowing what I was thinking.

"No, I pass right through the root. First my foot, then my leg, then my hand. I'm disappearing. He's making me disappear."

I tried not to show any thought on my face. By then, Valerie and I had already slept together twice in that doctor's cottage, and we'd laid in that narrow twin bed a long time naked and quiet. I remembered now that she'd pressed her fingers into me all over, kneading me like dough on my back and my chest. Patting like a blind person, she'd been making sure I was solid. Or that she was.

"I can't let him make me disappear. So when he's gotten tired of stooping and sits on that root now with his legs dangling close, I go to them and reach. I expect my hand to go through but it doesn't, so I untie the laces of his terrible preppy shoes and let them drop in the water. He's paying attention now, so I reach up and pull at his shirt and pull at his pants and pull him to be naked like me in the river. I have my arms around his neck when we fall backward off that oak root, and the water tries to squeeze between us but it can't. I slide my hands up his back, and I whisper, 'Why didn't you come with me?' "

I looked up, but she didn't notice.

"He sputters, trying to say something. I can feel him getting hard, and I know he won't hear me anymore, not like he used to, that I'd always be invisible to him from then on. The rope from the tree isn't far behind us, and I manage to reach it with the very tips of my fingers. I twist the loop at the end around his neck and shove him as deep under the water as I can."

My breath caught in my throat.

"My knee's on his back, squishing in, solid now. The harder I pull on the rope, the more solid I feel. He tries to flail his arms back, but they can't reach far enough to get me. They stop after a while, and I let him drift off down the river, free."

I'm not sure where they go. Sometimes during the day, I walk out to the corner of the fence where they pass through and I curl my fingers in the chain links. From what I can see from this side, about fifty yards of palmetto lead in a winding path to a stand of Australian pines. Of course, they leave no footprints, and where they go after that, there's no telling.

Once, I went around the outside of the fence to look around and I regretted it. The woods aren't right that way, when I cheat. Sure, it's dark in there and the pine needles crackle beneath my feet and the wind whooshes through the treetops, but all I see are old Styrofoam cups blown in from the highway and a toppled refrigerator dumped here long ago.

There's nobody there when I walk around the fence. The only way is through.

Almost everybody at the Wood liked to pretend they killed somebody. We had one guy who said he'd shot a Hells Angel with a spear gun from the wall of a seaside bar, and another who claimed he'd been a back-up trigger man at the Kennedy assassination, assigned to a manhole in Dealy Plaza. To hear them tell it, they were all farm-league Mansons.

So I wasn't sure I believed Valerie. She enjoyed embellishing reality a little too much to be entirely credible, for one thing. For another, she was about five foot six and a hundred and thirty pounds, not someone I could envision drowning a strapping frat boy. Of course, I'd seen her naked by then, thin and long beneath me, and nobody naked looks like a killer.

But I checked anyway, visiting a few nearby libraries to scan through back issues of the local papers, looking for mention of bodies floating up out of the Peace or Manatee rivers. I wasn't surprised or unsurprised when I discovered an obituary for a Benjamin Farrell, found tangled in mangrove roots twenty miles down the river from his hometown. The body had been badly mutilated by animals of some kind, maybe alligators, and the cause of death was indeterminate. The going theory was that he'd drowned while swinging drunk into the water late one night as the kids often did, though nobody could convince any of Ben's friends to admit they'd been with him. Valerie had gotten lucky.

I thought that finding out that she killed someone would inhibit our relationship, but somehow it was just the opposite. I'm not saying I was turned on by what she did, not even excited or sympathetic; there wasn't much of that left in me. But we walked out along the fence even more often, sneaking into our cottage or the west entrance guard shack or the vehicle barn for the talk therapy that mattered—the silent kind, sweaty and wide-eyed.

Our sessions in my office, the official ones that required reports and diagnoses, took on a quiet and comfortable quality, like retirees at home after fifty years of marriage. Our conversation was casual and funny. We shared little stories of our lives. Sometimes she read aloud to me or I to her.

I remember she read from *Grapes of Wrath*, that section with Muley Graves. He was the nutty ranch hand who stayed behind when the Joads lit out for California, lurking in the abandoned barn like a feral cat. He gets swallowed by the tractors when the banks come to take the land.

"I'd stick around, too," she told me.

"What for?" I asked.

She shrugged beside me; we'd gotten bold enough to sit together on the couch sometimes. She'd fallen asleep on my shoulder once, even. "Maybe because someone's got to see what happens next. To see things to the end. Like how every funeral has to have one guy who watches."

"Huh," was all I said. I imagined that Muley Graves was a paranoid schizophrenic, with the foreclosure of the farm as a triggering event for a lengthy episode. He saw himself as the last defender of the castle, a classic delusion. I didn't tell her that, though.

"I never want to be one of those people who takes the hint, you know? Who leaves when you want her to."

Not much worry of that, I figured.

Valerie and I tried our best to be discreet, but we were never quite sure who knew about us and who didn't. There were a hundred patients on each ward during the Wood's peak population, and way too few case workers—an average of one for every thirty or forty patients, each with complicated case histories to maintain. There were even fewer actual doctors, and most of them came in once a week from neighboring towns to write the prescriptions we recommended with a cursory flip through the files.

It was a situation both helpful and harmful to our relationship. On the one hand, almost nobody was watching if you took a walk with your patient in the fields. On the other, the few that were would find it suspicious that you'd take that extra time with one of your forty cases.

Doctor Federovich turned out to be the latter type, of course.

"Don't get too used to her," he said one day passing me on the ward.

I stopped but he didn't. That was all the confirmation he needed.

"You won't be here long," he said over his shoulder. "Neither will she."

~

Oh, she's still here. So am I, in my way.

When people stumble on the Wood today, they can't always tell what it was. It didn't look much like a mental hospital even when it was one—no bars on the windows or anything, no rooms full of scary wires or restraints—and now it could be a bunch of old warehouses.

A guy from the county comes out maybe once every couple of months to drive around on his tractor in big reckless circles, missing huge patches of weeds but doing well enough to keep it looking good from the road. Sometimes kids will park their cars by the old front gate at night, sometimes to neck and other times to scare themselves with the idea of madmen electroshocked to death or madwomen driven to suicide. They roll down their windows, trying to listen over their own giggles and shushes, and I'm always so very tempted to make the mournful wail they're waiting for.

They sent a couple of detectives once to find me. Well, not me specifically, just the source of the lights people sometimes report seeing from the highway. I guess those are scary when you're driving by yourself on a dark road, expecting your own headlights to be the only illumination in miles of black. It can't be my lantern they see; the porch doesn't even face that way. Maybe they see the flow of that long bluish stream of patients slithering through the field. If I saw that from inside a car, I'd call the cops, too.

The cops poked around in the doctors' cottages. They opened closets, flipped through my paperbacks, tried all the light switches, sniffed around in the bedrooms to see if someone had been sleeping there. I keep a pretty clean house; it's hard to tell I live there, which come to think of it, isn't all that different from how I lived back in the regular world.

They swaggered between the old hospital buildings, cupping their hands to look in the windows. They jiggled the door handle to the cafeteria, one of three doors that are still locked. They squinted off into the woods, right at the spot in the fence where the figures go through, but they were comfortable enough still to light cigarettes before heading back to the unmarked cruiser.

I wouldn't find out what Federovich meant until a staff meeting two weeks later. That was when, seated at the end of the table in his ceremonial lab coat with his hands folded, he told us soberly that the state was closing down the Wood by the end of August, six months away.

"The official word isn't coming until next week, but I thought you might like to know in advance, perhaps to make arrangements." He paused, not looking at us but somewhere in the upper corner of the room. "I trust that you'll keep this confidential from the clients in the meantime."

Right, I thought. The staff had worse poker faces than the patients. Everyone started talking at once, not quite to anybody specific but loud enough that anyone within about fifty feet of the conference room would hear.

"You've done good work," said Federovich, glancing around at everybody but skipping over me. "And

I assure you that the state will do everything it can to place you in other positions where you can continue to do so."

"What are we doing with the clients?" I asked, careful to use Federovich's term. I'd called them "wackos" once and gotten written up for it.

Everyone looked at me, probably surprised I'd asked the question.

"There are two options, of course: release to community care or transfer to Chattahoochee."

Chattahoochee was another state institution with higher security than ours. It was far closer to everybody's image of a mental hospital, one with bars in the windows and screaming behind the doors. It was where the dangerous and hopeless went.

"Of course, nobody's funding the halfway houses any more than they funded us, so there's no telling how many of the clients we release there are going to get care at all after a few months. I expect some will end up in jail or homeless."

He said it so matter-of-factly. I might have heard it matter-of-factly, too, if I hadn't been sleeping with one of them.

"So treat 'em and street 'em?" I said, saying aloud in a meeting what so many of us had grumbled for years.

Federovich didn't blink. If he saw one bright side to closing the Wood, it was that I'd be out of the mental health care field however long it took to find a job, maybe forever. "Essentially, yes. Our task now is to classify the clients based upon their suitability for community release. For the chronic or dangerous cases, of course, there's nothing but Chattahoochee. I'm establishing a board for the final determinations based upon all your recommendations."

So my choice, not really a choice at all, was to send Valerie to Chattahoochee or release her back to the world. Would she kill someone else? I doubted it; nobody had that emotional import in her life anymore, not even me, and nobody would again. But I knew she wasn't finished with whatever she was becoming.

I made the mistake of hurrying her.

~

It gets stormy in the summer here, and violent gray thunderheads gather in the afternoons like a herd of buffalo. If it gets too bad, I go into the old ward building and curl up on that green couch in my office. I don't do it often because of the noises.

The ward is full of whispers at night, and the horrible government tile just passes them from one end of the building to the other. A mumble at the far door can sound like Valerie purring in my ear, though it never is.

It's just a myth that ghosts scream and wail. They mutter, making you strain to hear, just like the patients used to.

~

I'll admit I entertained the fantasy of keeping Valerie. I'd find some way to "cure" her and we'd drive away from the gates of Worthington Wood to get married at the courthouse. She'd have her matching suitcases in the back of my car, and we'd go off and drive somewhere forever. Somewhere that didn't scare her, where she saw nothing.

I think the surest sign of love is the need for a road trip together. I wanted to see Valerie seeing Pigeon Forge, the Alamo, the Grand Canyon, the world's biggest ball of yarn, and a hundred Waffle Houses and Cracker Barrels in between. Something had happened to her the last time she took that trip, and I wanted something to happen to me, too. It hadn't in such a long time, and maybe she had some to spare.

So the priority in those last months was fixing her. There are strategies we were supposed to follow, a checklist of guilt and remorse, but the first logical step was to stop sleeping with her. It could only help to isolate the variables of whatever was wrong, after all.

"Come *on*," she said a few days after my unspoken decision. She tried to pull me from my office chair and instead it squeaked forward and thumped against the desk. "What's the matter with you?"

I planted my feet to go no further. "We never talk anymore," I said.

"Sure we do. In the good way."

"No," I said. "I mean, I don't think I'm helping you."

She bent over me, both hands on the arms of my chair, her hair hanging in my face. "Are you trying to *fix* me?"

"Why else are you here?" I replied.

She stood up, smiling wryly. "For the company," she said. Then she shook her head. "It's sweet, it really is. Probably something to do with guilt, am I right? You've screwed a patient and now you have to make her not a patient anymore."

I hadn't thought about it that deeply, but yeah, maybe that was part of it. But not all.

"We may not have all the time we think we do," I said.

"They're closing down the hospital."

See? The patients probably knew before we did.

"Well, that's part of it, yeah," I said. "But, even if the Wood was here forever, you wouldn't want to stay, right?"

"Why not?"

"Because this is a mental institution, Valerie. It does things to people."

"So does the rest of the world," she said. Then, more quietly, she added, "I'm more solid here than most places."

"Valerie—"

"I have a theory about crazy people," she said.

Most of them do. "Really."

"Really," she said. "I think the people everyone else calls 'crazy' are drifting from this world to another one. Slipping between the cracks, sort of. And not all of their brain goes into the other world at once and it can talk to the other part that doesn't and it says things neither side can understand."

That was a popular theory with the wackos, that they were visionaries seeing into some other quanta of reality or the realm of Faerie or whatever. My heart sank to hear her say it because it was even more proof that she'd taken too much of the Wood to heart. Now she too was addicted to epiphany.

"How much of your brain is here and how much is there?" I asked.

"It's not the brain you should be worried about," she said.

She meant the spirit, I assumed. Another favorite theory was that the Wood blunted the edges of the soul, wearing people thinner and thinner until they didn't exist anymore. The wackos liked that one because it offered an upside to being cut loose thanks to psychiatric facility defunding.

Valerie opened the DSM, our venerable handbook of just what the hell goes wrong with people. "Or maybe I'm just schizophrenic?"

The idea had occurred to me. Delusions, disorganized speech and thought...mild, certainly, but present all the same.

"Oh, wait. How about Narcissistic Personality Disorder? 'Grandiose sense of self-importance,' check. 'Believes that he or she is special,' check. 'Sick and tired of the world not mattering to her,' check and double-check."

I'd thought of that one, too. Also Schizoid Personality Disorder and Antisocial Personality Disorder. Lack of feeling for others, flat aspect, delusional fixations, self-absorption—I mean, worse than the rest of us.

"You know what I think it is?"

She sat on my desk, knocking things over with her bare knees to sit Indian-style a few feet away from me, her gown high. "Ooh! You've cured me!"

"I think you've got 'Shit-or-get-off-the-pot-ism.'"

"Huh," she said. "Is that in the index?"

"No. It's a common affliction of people with higher-than-average intelligence who don't see any meaning in the world, no purpose, so they wait for it to manifest. Of course, it never does...and so they keep retreating and retreating inward."

"Until they disappear," she said.

"Yeah, that's a word for it," I replied. "They don't realize that to be solid, you have to do things. You have to be meaning yourself."

Valerie's eyes narrowed. "That's the stupidest thing I ever heard."

And that was the most hostile thing she'd ever said, so I thought I was on the right track. I pressed some more.

"I'll tell you the stupidest thing I've ever heard." I could hear myself talking but it didn't quite sound like me. "The stupidest thing I've ever heard is that a smart and beautiful woman can't get past the ninth-grade idea that the world is a sham hardly worth her intelligence. Everybody with an I.Q. over a hundred thinks that, and maybe a few of them are right. You know what they do?"

Valerie folded her arms and gazed over my shoulder out the window. "What do they do?"

"They fake it. They play along. And then they live what they love some other way, writing or drawing or building birdhouses or calling into talk radio shows when no one else is looking. They stop staring at their feet too much to walk"

"Fake it," said Valerie. "Play along. That's a great idea. I never thought of that. Maybe I can do what you've done, living out your imaginative fantasy existence in this awful little office at this awful little mental hospital. It's a bravura performance, your faking."

"Yeah, I know. That's why I'm qualified to tell you all this. You think I've never felt like I'm fading? All my life, I've always been empty, like my feelings don't go deep enough. My mother died and I was empty. My wives left me and I was empty. I was empty on drugs and empty in therapy. You're the first thing that fills me up and makes me solid, but that's only a metaphor, right? I've always been real, you've always been real." I reached for her hands but she pulled them away. "You helped me figure that out."

"I'm glad my therapy is working out for you," she said. "Come talk to me when you really get it."

I blocked her from getting up. "Valerie, they're trying to decide what to do with you. The two choices are a halfway house or Chattahoochee. Neither of them is good. Once you're in the system, you never get out. They just keep caring about you less."

"Wow," she said. "That's almost worth seeing, like absolute zero."

"I care about you—"

"You care about me? You *care* about me? You know what? Go to hell. You don't care about me. You care about the idea of me, the idea of what I can be for you. A magical crazy fairy to sprinkle life dust in your life or something." She slid herself off my desk with a crash of papers and file folders. "I liked you better when you didn't talk."

She was turning to leave and I grabbed at her arm. She swatted back to knock me away. Somehow, though we were a foot apart, we missed. But we couldn't have missed. We passed right through one another, our limbs phantoms.

We were both surprised, not just by the miss but by the cold, sharp pain in our hands where they should have touched. She walked backwards, shaking her head with a smile on her face and looking around. She reached for the shelf of reference books but pulled back. She reached for the wall to steady herself, but she pulled back from there, too.

"I'm fading," she said.

She backed toward the door. I wondered as she fell silent if she was thinking of killing me, just to see which one of us was real. I wondered why I hoped it would be her.

I break windows these days for fun. I'll roll my sleeve down over my fist and pop it through the panes of glass. Some of them are reinforced by a thin crosshatch of wire, but even those bulge inward with a satisfying spray of clear pebbles. I'm all the happier if I slice into my arm because blood...well, blood is solid.

That's why they move furniture around the wards, why they slam the doors. They're testing if they're solid anymore. When I punch a tree sometimes and it doesn't always hurt, I get my answer.

~

The last days at the Wood were like the fall of an empire: the conquered people growing restless and bold, the conquerors nervous and checking their watches. Things were never too orderly at the Wood even during the good days, but those end weeks slipped into chaos: patients sleeping in rooms that weren't theirs, groups staying up all night in the day room, people missing meals and sometimes even meds. We were down to two nurses per shift and one visiting doctor, plus two psychologists. I was one, to Federovich's annoyance; everyone else had taken new jobs. I wasn't looking.

Some fifty patients remained, all of "pending status." The others had gone off to community care or Chattahoochee, and even a few off to prison. The ones still around had family issues, nobody knowing if they could be released and where. They were easy to ignore—easier, I mean, even than they had been—parked quietly in their day room chairs. Among them was Valerie, who'd murdered her boyfriend and gotten away with it.

She'd stopped coming to session and started palming her meds. She ate only breakfast. She grew thinner and more drab, the kind of person I could see only in the corner of my eye. And she'd never look at me.

Valerie was making her choice for good now, and she was showing the others how to do it, too. They sat together in their dressing gowns in the day room, staring at the television. They smoked cigarettes once an hour on the patio. They whispered amongst themselves, and they looked over their shoulders at us with grins. They'd walk together in pairs, swinging their clasped hands high to the front and then high to the back, not caring if anyone was in the way.

She was teaching them, I know now: teaching them to be invisible. They gave us no trouble, which in itself proved to be a kind of trouble in the end.

For my final determination, I thought of trying reverse psychology on Federovich, giving him something to overrule one last time. But I couldn't bring myself to write anything but "community care" on the recommended disposition line.

Federovich chose Chattahoochee for her instead.

"It's too late," he told me, closing her folder after the committee meeting. "You all but say it in your report. She's institutionalized now, shutting down. Whatever you talked about with her, whatever you did in those sessions—it didn't work. Your last patient intervention was a failure. I can't say it much bucks the pattern."

Oh, it did, I wanted to say. Valerie was never part of a pattern. But I didn't say anything, didn't mention she might even be worse than he thought. It was another of my little cowardices.

I sleep very little these days; I just don't need it. Mostly, I watch and listen, maybe waiting for those tractors to come and take me like they did Muley Graves. Valerie left all her books behind and I read that chapter every so often, trying to figure out if he was real or not, if he had a choice at all but to stay where things were firm.

Valerie and the other final fifty patients disappeared on May 2, 1998, sometime between 11:08PM and 11:14PM, if the security cameras are anything to go by. The nurse on shift left Valerie and a few others staring blankly at the television news for a quick smoke, never leaving earshot of the chuckling weatherman. She got a cold feeling, though, so she stamped out her cigarette half-finished and leaned back inside. The day room was empty.

So were the rooms. And the cafeteria. And the grounds, according to the security guards as they patrolled in their whirring golf carts with melodramatic badges on the sides.

In six minutes, Valerie and the others had wordlessly made their great escape. All of the doors were locked. No one found a tunnel or a hatch. The patients left all their things behind, sometimes even the gowns in which they'd been sleeping. A few made their beds first. One left a tip for the janitor.

The cameras showed static.

Federovich was incensed: he'd taken a position at a far more respectable hospital in another state, and word that he'd lost fifty human beings with questionable legal standing didn't keep him the job long enough even to move there. With the help of three county sheriff's departments and the Florida Department of Law Enforcement, he tried to track them down in every direction, probably to redeem himself.

Men rumbled across the yellow grass fields in ATVs or clopped down dirt roads on horseback. Helicopters made the palmetto fronds dance and shiver. Divers checked the ponds and creeks; I told them that the old swinging rope at the boat ramp might be a good place. In the end, they found nothing.

The epiphany to which I'm addicted now is that people get less real the less you listen to them. That's what ghosts are, right? People to whom nobody listened, people lingering to find someone who will? I don't know if they're dead or alive or whatever, but I know something comes unanchored when we ignore them.

I saw it all the time in those corridors on the ward, living doctors and nurses breezing by the gowned specters standing in doorways or slumped in chairs by the TV. How many people had I walked through with nothing but a shudder? How many people were edges to me, not quite alive?

The whole world's a ghost factory. We all fade like the paint on these buildings, sometimes from too much sun, sometimes from too little. We blur and blend to the murky shades left behind when something vivid dies.

And now, except for your attention, I'm one of them.

I wasn't useless in those last days at the Wood, whatever Federovich said. I wrote the reports he demanded, affirming that none of those missing would be dangerous, for one thing. For another, I helped the security guard lower and fold the flag on the last day, wide and blue and loud with insect cries from the woods.

I drove slowly outside that gate, the second-to-last car before the state inspector. I rolled down the windows and took a road trip to a nearby town for supplies. I returned by night, knifed all four of my tires in a shaded glen of pines far from the road, and came home. Here.

I'm going to stop writing now. They're coming through almost every night, the ribbon of spirits, winding between the old concrete buildings toward the woods. Always the woods, those Australian pines where it's always a little chill and cloudy, where it's quiet enough for their whispers to keep each other so slightly anchored to our world.

I'm going to stop writing now and leave this for you, whoever you are. A transient? One of those cops? The guy driving that bulldozer at Muley Graves? It doesn't matter. Your attention will come too late to make me solid, to stop me from passing through the fence to join them, but I thought someone should know. All crazy people think that, don't they?

I'm going to take her hand as best I can, and then I'm going to listen until we're both real again. Even if it takes forever.

Burying the Hatchets

Miss Corwin was ahead of her time, or maybe behind her time, or maybe from another time altogether. It's a miracle that it took them so long to run her out of town because that's how I had a chance to have her as a teacher.

She saved me from being an asshole. She saved all of us.

We were a class of big personalities, I guess. Ronnie Tolcolm is in the U.S. House of Representatives now, for instance. Junie DeVera is a state prosecutor. Wendy Niels was in the movies for a decade. And not one, not two, but three of us ended up being big mouths on TV: Henry Young was a big star on that sitcom *These Children Are Monsters*, Violet Dorwell has that cooking show, and I'm a political correspondent for CBS.

If you told me then that I'd be a political correspondent for CBS, I'd have tried very hard to shoot myself with my pearl-handled Roy Rogers pistols. Failing that, I would have clubbed myself to death with them.

But yeah, big personalities. Loud kids. Verbal kids. Kids who'd been told a little too often that they had bright futures ahead of them. Kids that you're only supposed to have one of in each class.

So we were mean. You could write a paper on how mean we were, something about "establishing norms in a simian group." We fought for attention in the way kids know best: with relentless mockery and bullying. I don't mean physical bullying; we had too much to lose for that. I mean the endless sniping of children, taking aim at any weakness and firing every verbal bullet they have.

When Violet got tested for Gifted and ended up back in our class, we called her "One Point Shy." When Henry beaned himself on the swing set in the recess yard, we all talked the rest of the day in gibberish to make him think he'd gotten a concussion. When Junie accidentally got two milks for lunch instead of one, we told her that she could never be a lawyer now because the courts make you pinky swear that you never, ever stole anything.

It doesn't sound so bad, but that kind of thing escalates, I guess. Each new cruelty has to be a little worse than the last for it to have the same effect. You didn't win if someone didn't cry.

We hit the top of our game one morning when Wendy came to school.

She arrived every morning in her father's fancy black convertible. He liked to drive with the top down, slowly following the curve of the sidewalk so everybody could see us, steering that thing like he was a sea captain. Sometimes he even wore one of those hats with the anchor on the front. Nobody was quite sure what he did for a living: "Probably counts his money," was my mother's best guess.

He'd stop in front of all of us, put his arm around Wendy, and give her a big kiss so we all could see. Sometimes we'd make smooching sounds after he drove away, and she'd duck between us to get to class.

I have no idea what was different that day. All I can think of is that I saw her flinch very slightly, you know? Or saw something in her eyes? All I do know is that I felt this electricity from my fingers to my brain, the surge that comes right before doing something incredible...or terrible.

Before I even thought of it, I fired what I thought would be the coolest and most devastating salvo ever.

"Hey, Wendy," I said, all sing-song. "When ya gonna marry your father? When ya gonna have babies?"

A laugh started through the crowd but cut short when Wendy just...collapsed. Down she went, from standing to a puddle on the ground, crying in a way that I've never heard since and never want to again. It was cosmic, that crying—the kind you do when you don't think you'll ever stop.

And she didn't, at least for a long time. We stopped laughing, but she wept and wept and wept for the whole morning. Miss Corwin had to take her to the school nurse, and we saw her go away in an ambulance.

What I didn't know was that Wendy's father was interested in doing worse than marrying her, that he'd tried plenty worse, and I was the one who picked away the heavy scab she'd built to protect herself when he wasn't around.

I didn't know all the details then; they came out later, slowly, over the rest of our schooling. But right then I knew I'd won the game for all time, and I knew it made me sick.

When Miss Corwin came back from the nurse without Wendy, she entered the room with her heels clicking sharply on the tile floor. She slammed the door behind her and pointed to our desks. "Everybody sit!" she bellowed.

We did, quickly. Some of us folded our hands because it made us look more studious and considerate. I wasn't sure I should bother, but it gave them something to do other than shake from what I'd done.

"Enough," she said to us. "This is enough, don't you think?"

We all looked around at one another.

"Close your eyes," Miss Corwin commanded.

Our eyes flickered a few at a time, but all of us did.

"Raise your arms to your sides, like a biplane," she commanded next.

We did. In the darkness behind my eyes, my arms felt heavy and wobbly.

"Your arms are antennas," she said. "Like for radio. But instead of radio, they can feel meanness. Do you feel that?"

Nobody said anything.

"Don't think about it. Feel it. Doesn't it feel cold, sharp? Can you feel it blowing against your skin? It's swirling around. It's been swirling around for years, all that meanness you spit at each other, all that cruelty."

A few of the others giggled, but I didn't. I could feel that meanness, maybe because I worried that my antenna transmitted as well as received. My arms seemed to move back slightly from the pressure.

"Keep your eyes closed tight. Squish them hard until you see that purple line all surrounded by stars."

I did and I saw it.

"Now imagine an animal. Don't think too hard about it! Just an animal, any animal. It'll come to you from the distance if you're quiet."

I waited. I scanned from side to side on the other side of my eyelids. I stared at the flickering horizon but nothing came.

"Nobody's coming," said Ronnie.

"Shhh," said Miss Corwin.

"Mine isn't an animal. It's a letter," said Henry.

"Shhh," said Miss Corwin again.

My arms were growing tired and my attention wavered from the blackened plain before my eyes. That was when I saw it ambling from one corner, zig-zagging, pausing to sniff the ground: a buck with a small rack of antlers. It clopped through the darkness and I stood very still, sat very still, as it came closer. Its nose nudged against my face, and its wide brown eye peered into mine.

"That's your animal," said Miss Corwin quietly. "The animal that guides you when you listen deeply enough. It only comes when you're quiet, when you don't quite look directly at it."

A deer? I was a deer? I was disappointed it wasn't a lion or a shark or something.

Many more minutes seemed to pass before she finally said, "Now lower your arms and open your eyes."

The room was brighter now, certainly, but also more peaceful. Blood rushed back from my body to my arms, and I felt light-headed.

"What do you think your animal would have said to Wendy this morning?" she asked us.

"Animals don't talk," said Violet.

"Well, that's a start, isn't it?" Miss Corwin started pulling down the boxes of art supplies. "This afternoon we are building masks for our spirit animals so we can become them whenever we want. And then we're having a funeral."

A funeral? I have to admit I assumed it was mine. If I was the source of that words that snapped Wendy's brain, it made sense that I was the bad apple that had to be pulled from the barrel.

But even though I was scared, I spent the day with paste and scissors, felt and newspaper, buttons and cardboard. I made something like a deer, I guess, jabbing two twigs into the top of my paper-mache head. I painted it a dull brown with black-rimmed eyes.

It was the afternoon by the time we finished. Miss Corwin had been gone from the room for close to an hour, but none of us had noticed; we'd been too focused on our work.

"Let's go," she said quietly, leaning in the door.

We followed, some of us putting on our masks or wearing them like hats. We snaked our way through the hallways past incredulous students. Some of them opened their mouths to make fun of us, but nothing ever seemed to come out. Principal Bowers raised his hand to get Miss Corwin's attention, but she walked right by him.

In the recess yard, Miss Corwin led us to a rectangular hole by the oak tree the forestry club had planted last year.

"Now lean in and scream," she said.

We looked at her like she was crazy.

"We'll start with you," she said, steering me by the shoulders to the hole.

This was it, I thought: she's shoving me in.

Her face hovered behind my ear. "Just crouch down and scream into the ground. Scream everything mean you've ever said, everything mean you've ever heard, all the things you hate, all the things you wish were different."

I stooped slightly and growled.

"That's not a yell. Clench your fists if you have to. Bare your teeth."

I tried again, closing my eyes, teetering at the edge on my haunches. I screamed, God I screamed. They tell me that you could hear me yelling about my father's death in the War, about my step-father, about my older sister, about all the times I'd felt stupid or alone. It was like throwing up: you could feel the poison in your throat but you knew it was going away.

By the time I opened my eyes, I'd fallen in. Dazed, I reached to climb out and Miss Corwin pulled me up.

"See?" she said.

I nodded, stunned. I stumbled behind the others, knocking into them with my antlers, my vision still blurry.

And the others, one by one, did the same. They screamed. They cried. They shouted. They swore—God, Ronnie swore so horribly that Principal Bowen came running out with a blanket to cover him but Miss Corwin held him back.

When the last of us had screamed, Miss Corwin handed us the shovels. "Now we bury all that forever."

Shovel by shovel, scoop by scoop, we filled in the hole. That was the lightest soil I've ever pitched in my life; I felt like Superman flipping it back in. I almost smiled like the others, but I figured it wasn't time yet.

It's funny, but we were sure a lot nicer to one another after that. I even took Wendy to the spring formal a few years later.

And after school, things were different for all of us. A lot of lawyers came out of that bunch, the good kind, and a lot of reporters, too. A lot of people who look at terrible things and try to stop them without raising their voices.

I've seen those terrible things as a reporter. I followed a war a hundred times more vicious than the one my father died in. I've seen charred bodies and men screaming. I could have been angry scores of times, could have picked up a rifle and jabbed a bayonet into someone. But my animal was always with me and my anger wasn't. I thank Miss Corwin for that.

What's funny is that when I've been back to my hometown for reunions, I've always driven by that tree. The leaves closest to the bottom are still black, but they get greener the closer they are to the sky.

Universicule

It's amazing, Charlotte, this book; it's everything we hoped. To call it MS 719 like someone's old diary or account book is a staggering failure of representation, but then, so are all our other symbols. Better to give it a number so as not to imply we've even come close.

The librarian here—built with maximum utility in some Librarianwerks, it seems, bun tightened and oiled daily—took me into the vault to see it with great pomp and ceremony. First, I had to sign a massive and ancient ledger, my name just three or four rows down from luminaries like Kimball and Junas-Smith. Then she handed me white cotton gloves and a surgical mask, which I put on as she unlocked two massive doors with long codes on their electronic pads.

The second door opened with a rush of stale air and the motion-sensitive lights ignited one tube after the other, revealing rows of metal drawers like safety deposit boxes. We clomped down to one on the far end, our steps echoing on the elevated floor, and she turned two keys simultaneously to open it. Out came a stainless steel drawer, and from that came a stainless steel tray, and from that came a cloth-wrapped bundle.

She set it on the research table against the wall, gently peeled back the cloth, and motioned me to the only chair. She lingered a moment to watch me open the leather-bound volume and turn the first few pages with motions so slow that it was hard to tell they were motions. Satisfied, she nodded once and withdrew backwards from the tiny room.

Leaving me alone with it.

As we guessed, MS 719 is written on twenty parchment quires of eight leaves each, totaling 320 pages. From what I could tell from the hue of the paper and the discoloration of the ink, it was written sometime between 1590 and 1650; there was no hope of getting a sample for chemical analysis, given the security cameras. If I'd tried, the librarian would certainly have rushed in to cut off my hand.

The words on each page, if they are words, scroll from left to right in a soothing shade of brown. The handwriting is consistent throughout, something far more visible with the eye than the camera. The lettering precisely aligns on both the X and Y axes, as though written on an invisible grid. The letters range from recognizable characters of Early Modern English to tiny drawings of astrolabes and schooners, from geometric shapes to hieroglyphs.

The illustrations...well, they simply transcend human imagination. Plants and animals beyond conception (oh, don't make that face when I use that phrase), landscapes of lava, ocean cities, forests thick with peeking faces. On one page, I saw something like those guns from *Star Trek*. On another, a circuit diagram or maybe a subway map—it's hard to tell which.

We've seen pictures of it before, of course, but here in person, smelling this loamy garden of a book—God, you could plant seeds inside it and they'd grow trees of glass and gold with absinthe fruit.

I know, I know: you're so much more the theory geek and I the bibliographic one; you want to know more about what the book *means* (or fails to mean, or means to fail, or some other semantic sleight of hand). Well, love, without you here behind me, reading Kristeva on your stomach, bare legs folded, your tongue poking out a mere centimeter from your lips, I don't always remember to think about those things. You'll just have to fly the 4,400 miles to come over to England and remind me.

I hope the dissertation defense preparation is going well and your headlong battle with (or for) linguistic entropy continues apace. Of course I miss you, and not just because all these signs and menus over here need Deconstructing.

And, though you loathe seeing it in print because its meaning slips hopelessly through the interstices of signifiers and signifieds, I love you.

I would hardly call my interest in MS 719 "fetishistic," especially when you, Charlotte, are by far my most consistent one. Perhaps it is better to say I am "interested," "fascinated," or even—temporarily, academically—"obsessed." I'll admit I've dreamed about the book, but that's hardly surprising given how far I've come to see it, how many adjustments and sacrifices we made to get me here. They aren't bad dreams, either, so don't be so worried about me.

Today, I started the process of doing what the CIA, NSA, SIS, Mossad, and probably three hundred eminent scholars of literature or computer science have failed to do: *read* MS 719. I think the problem lies in the *shape* of those letters. They too easily invite comparisons to a code, and all my esteemed predecessors have pursued their task with the grim cheerlessness of cryptographers. They miss entirely the fluidity and poetry of language qua language.

Or at least that's what I'll write in my paper. For you, my Sweet, the truth: working under the theory that immersion would help, I sat all day and stared at it.

For the eight working hours of the antiquities collection, I turned pages and stared at them, inviting the book to seep into my consciousness. Having no way to independently measure my consciousness, I cannot tell if it is fuller or heavier today than yesterday, though I'm awfully tired. The Librarianatrix found me dozing beside the book and sternly rapped her key on the steel table to wake me up. That probably won't do much for my scholarly reputation.

Maybe I can balance that out with all that I've learned about the book's origin. I've consulted a handful of monographs, at least one of them written by what we'd almost certainly call a "crackpot," but they all agree on a few simple facts. MS 719 was found among seized art objects in a Nazi storage vault, deep within an abandoned Polish salt mine. Among the priceless sculptures and paintings from all over the world—Etruscan statuary, Renaissance paintings, sketches by Michelangelo—it was easy to ignore a book full of crazy symbols. The tale goes that one of the Russian soldiers simply gave it to a curious British officer, one David Mawley, in exchange for...nobody knows. Likely rations or liquor.

For the next ten years, MS 719's journey is less clear. Some hypothesize that Lt. Mawley tried selling it to a variety of collectors, most of them the unscrupulous sorts who hoard artifacts for themselves just to own little leverage points of history. Names like Oliver Grandin come up here, who you know as the publisher of those fake letters from Joyce to Hemingway. Even Mawley, though, knew better than to sell to the likes of him, and eventually the book found its way here to the British Library in the mid-1960s. Donated, no less. With a brief letter saying, "Good luck. Don't read more than three pages in a sitting."

Yes, donated. That proves to be a double-edged sword, scholarship-wise: does it mean that the book is certainly a hoax because it was given so freely, or does it mean that the book is certainly not a hoax because there was no profit motive? I know what you'd say, that all books are hoaxes, that "authenticity" is a false pursuit, that all texts exist independently of their authors. Well, maybe. But it doesn't help legitimize the book any, or its study.

It also doesn't help the cause of scholarship that Leonard Nimoy had to come snooping around with his *In Search Of* cameras, ready to intone that this was clearly an alchemical journal or Shakespeare's opium dream or an ancient alien textbook left behind to spark the Age of Reason. You'd think a man with a butterfly collar that wide wouldn't get so much credibility, but there are always those tabloid-reading New Agers who will buy pretty much anything. In an experiment, they placed MS 719 beneath a glass pyramid for forty-eight hours and—to the amazement of no one with a high school science education—it came out warm to the touch.

Yeah, the greenhouse effect is funny that way.

So the British have kept it locked up ever since. There's nothing so ruinous to a reputation as an interview for a credulous 1970s TV show; those memories have lasted long here and the curators are reluctant to let anyone look at it again. Up until now, MS 719 appealed only to crazy people.

Oh, I can see you smirking. You know I'm not crazy, at least not in that way, and my research is an effort to defuse a mystery instead of perpetuate one. It's a simple book, I'm sure, somebody's jape, maybe a work of fiction. You've whispered your sweet nothings about the arbitrary meaning of all language too long for me to think anything else.

Really, we're working on the same thing. You're publishing the theory, and I'm publishing the research—the literal, concrete example of your grand totalizing concept that all our lives are but instantiations of our imagination.

I've tried instantiating you here by the powers of mine, but clearly I lack the chakra or mana of those New Age shamans. I have your totem fountain pen you gave me at graduation, but you are not in it. Perhaps I need to place it beneath a pyramid with MS 719.

Or maybe I simply need the warmth of your skin to do that much more pleasantly.

I love you, as always, and good "luck" on your defense next week. Instantiate them into amazement, Sweet.

Of course the defense went well. The committee was stacked with men who will be your disciples a few publications down the road—men who will teach your books to wide-eyed undergraduates asking what you're "really like." I can't wait to tell them that you do all your writing in your underwear. The best of it, anyway. As luck would have it, I do my best writing when you're in your underwear, too.

Like you, I have also made a significant stride forward. I have translated the first word of MS 719.

The word is *universicule.*

It was the label beneath a drawing of an atom, an object rendered with all the majesty of a galaxy. Whoever wrote this book clearly imagined that the universe really is "turtles all the way down," each small part somehow containing the whole. I'm reminded of those Mandelbrot sets, the fractal drawings that are the same at all their levels of magnification. The writer of MS 719 seems to have been far ahead of his (or her) time.

Universicule. Every atom portends the whole.

It's strange how dizzy and disoriented I am after each session with the book. It almost hurts to go outside again to the real world. Everything's too bright, and my feet hit the pavement too hard. Maybe they somehow change gravity in that crazy library along with the temperature and humidity.

I'm sorry to hear that you can't join me for the summer as we'd planned. I've tried not to let it unduly depress me, but, well, even MS 719 isn't as good a companion as you are. I understand completely, though, that you have conference papers to prepare and a grueling season of academic interviews ahead of you. Yet rational as I am, there's still something painful to it. I always expected your success, Sweet, though I didn't expect it would overtake us so soon.

Never mind me. There's always the fall (not to be confused with the Fall) and some of the best scholarly work is done by the depressed. It gives them something better to imagine.

As always, I love you.

~

You haven't asked, but I suspect you're curious of my methodology for translating MS 719. It isn't complicated: I've just spent enough time with the manuscript to have developed a *sense* of what it says. You like to say that the senses are mere determinations of language, and if this is so, the language of MS 719 should all but translate itself.

I'm not much closer to knowing just what MS 719 really *is*. A diary? A sketchbook? A science or medical text? There are drawings of many plants and animals, of course, along with diagrams of machines and celestial phenomena. Of course, astrology was an important "science" to people of this era, and this could well be some kind of Underbible, a book driving at the behindness of things.

I have discovered something curious, however: there is clearly a narrative winding through the pages, a story being told among the scientific extrapolations. Words are repeated, Jygren and Archa, and I think they may be names. Perhaps this is a travelogue, following some kind of quest. I've seen other proper nouns, words like Thuria and Ivbanth, that could well be the names of places or other people.

I've seen no indication, though, that these map to anything in our world. Even with the little biology and astronomy I know, these aren't our plants and they aren't our stars. There are no illustrations of people, either, so for all I know, Jygren and Archa aren't even human.

It's been awhile since I've heard from you. I've heard *of* you through mutual friends, namely Shari and Chris, and I suppose you're busy in these waning days of summer. These were always the best times at school, weren't they? When the undergraduates were few? I've always said the only problem with a university is all the students. I remember how we could walk together through the Plaza of the Americas or sneak off to cuddle in Library West, or how you'd sit Indian-style on the floor between stacks of books. There's a light in Gainesville in early August that somehow seems to glow from the pages of MS 719; maybe there's some of your instantiation, another footnote.

I don't even know if you've found a teaching position or if you plan to take a year for post-doctorate work. I know the English department could use the slave labor, and I could certainly use your company. You're all that kept me grounded there. As for here, well...

Anyway, I do so love you, even now. I hope you'll write.

~

I've tried to call. I've sent you e-mail. I've sent messages in Facebook, that odious arena of human vanity. All I see of you are pictures I'm not in. Which is just as well, because, hey, I'm not much to look at. Now more than ever when I'm cadaverously thin and grey.

My work with MS 719. Well, there's definitely a story in the manuscript, some kind of imaginative tour or adventure in which two lovers cross an alien landscape to reunite after the break-up of their spaceship. Yes, spaceship. There are clear references to aeronautical concepts, headings and degrees, cosmic radiation, ray guns. Monsters, even.

There are tender moments, too, when the distance between the words "Jygren" and "Archa" draws shorter than usual. The names then dance and oscillate in the text together, attracted particles on the same quantum of the universicule. That's when they're making love just like we used to do among our books on the apartment floor in our own alchemical attraction.

Then the names drift apart in the text and in come the prepositions, the before-positions, the speckled words of here and there. It's too early to tell whether Jygren and Archa return to each other's arms but how can they not? They live on the same plane, the same page, and all we need to do is fold reality to bring them back together.

Instantiation, as you say.

I don't like to be outside anymore. The Ivalia trees have taken on a grim aqua pallor, decidedly unhealthy and out of season, and the scavenging Dravshas seem restless in their sewer nests. The villagers look at me strangely, fascinated by my foreign clothes. I've tried to wear a Polwara in the local style, but it only serves to make me all the more obvious. I'm waiting at the door of the library for the very second it opens; at least there I have a room to myself.

I've missed you, my Sweet. A pen is not enough.

They're saying terrible things about me, these damned librarians, and you must not believe a word. Claiming I shout strange words in the marketplace. Alleging that I followed a woman to her Tsew, begging her to read a letter for me.

Worst of all, they accuse me of defacing MS 719. You've said more than once that the act of reading is a defacement, violating the perfect theoretical reading with a dirty, clumsy "real" one. Reading, writing. They're really the same act, according to you. Of course there are folds. Of course there are new words written in, yes, my browning blood that no longer pulses with yours. We're creating and re-creating in our mental house of mirrors, after all, and now MS 719 now lacks for nothing. It cost my blood to write it, to finish it, but they couldn't know the proper ending without me. They hadn't been immersed.

I'm glad your pen was sharp.

And what of Jygren and Archa? Of course their love is hopeless, like all love, merely because there's no reconciling the imagination with "the" reality. The last I heard, Archa had married another, somewhere in the center of the continent; it was her husband who told me, threatening that any more letters to his "wife" would be met with action from the law, as though the constables of western Heobrun have any jurisdiction in the east! He claimed in thuggish audacity that it had long been over between Jygren and Archa, years past, that she'd tried to be polite to her former mentor in fear for her academic career.

Mentor! Is that what we're calling lovers in the leaden slums of Heobrun these days? True, yes, I held your hand and led you through the rocky passes of Thuria. But you did not drag, my Sweet. You did not drag.

That doesn't matter now, I suppose. What matters is that I've read what no one else could, deciphered MS 719 and discovered its true nature. The manuscript is a love letter, of course, with no addressee and no addressor, infinitely interceptible, from and to nobody.

Acknowledgements

A veritable army of people helped birth this collection of stories, and because you've come here on your own volition, I'm going to come close to listing them all.

Get comfortable.

The literal physical product in your hand would not exist at all without Lethe Press Chairman and CEO Steve Berman's guidance and support. Beyond the logistics of publishing the book, however, Steve has always been a supportive confidant and friend throughout my writing career. Without Lethe's talented design czar Alex Jeffers, the book may well have appeared on your doorstep in overalls and a straw hat instead of in the elegant tuxedo and tails you see before you.

Thank you, also, to Jeff Ford for his introduction (both here and via his wonderful work). It's an honor to be even noticed by someone who has plumbed far deeper into the same wilderness that I love, much less recommended. Laird Barron and John Mantooth honor me, too, with their wonderful support for the book.

Old friends Norman Amemiya, William Simmons, Don Rochester, Tom Phillips, Ray Rodil, Thad Smith, Ed Ralph, Jason Carraway, Nell and Debbie Phillips, and Chris Harben have all listened to my campfire stories for years and lived to tell about it, so they deserve a hearty thanks (and congratulations). So too do new friends like Arnold Cassel and Kelley Vanda.

The weekly story-watching salons with Richard Soehner, Lillian Soehner, and Mac McDonald have been invaluable for improving my own writing. They've been fun, too.

Stonecoast MFA faculty Jim Kelly, Liz Hand, Mike Kimball, David Anthony Durham, Scott Wolven, and Nancy Holder read many of the stories here in early manuscript and graciously helped me make them worth your time. They've all been invaluable mentors and friends.

So too have fellow students at the Stonecoast program including Robert Stutts, Linda Daly, Angela Still, Zachary Jernigan, Meghan Sinoff, Tarver Nova, Adam Mills, Paul Kirsch, Ben Burgis, Nellie Dilger, Kevin St. Jarre, Laura Williams, Carolyn O'Doherty, Richard Cambridge, and Bix Skahill. Plus, hell, all the rest of you. Your continued presence in my life has made my whole life an MFA program...uh, in a good way.

Of course, I wouldn't have the oh-so-fertile psychological ground to write like this without my family: Dianne Hall, Andrew Hall, Karen and Marty Simpson, and Katie and Emily Simpson. I'm sincerely proud to be part of a family who thinks it is funny to put the tails from a mink stole in the gas cap of a car or the closed door of an oven.

It is an interesting coincidence that all of these stories (except the concept of "Prudenter to Dream") were written AFTER I met Aimee Payne. Could that have something to do with the warm, comfortable, and supportive environment for writing we've built together? Perhaps. For her, I'm most grateful of all...for ending at least one search.

Story Notes

In Search Of

You may have heard: I really liked the television show *In Search Of*, and it helped make me the weirdo capable of writing a whole book of stories like these.

Aside from the television show, this story comes from my only demand of the afterlife: a debriefing in which all of my questions are answered. I want someone to explain to me what happened in Dallas in 1963, who the Zodiac was, and what was swimming around in Loch Ness.

Failing that, I'll accept a nice delusional fugue in the last seconds of my cognition.

Originally appeared in the June 2008 issue of Alfred Hitchcock's Mystery Magazine.

Endless Encore

From time to time on my website, I challenge myself to write a story in one hour based on a stock photo or public domain illustration. I select the image, set a timer for an hour, and post whatever comes out of it on my website.

I've written about fifty stories this way now, and they are some of my most popular work.

Some of the best illustrations for the stories come from a woman named Elizabeth Shippen Green. She drew images for magazines and children's books of the early 20th century, and from what I can tell, she had an eye for the creepy-realistic, a common image somehow imbued with implications of something strange behind it.

Which might be a good description of my own work, at least how I hope it to be.

Originally appeared in the May 2012 Drabblecast *podcast.*

The Speed of Dreams

I was lucky enough in 2006 to meet a retired racing greyhound named Patti and have her come to live with me.

She seemed to enjoy our afternoon naps best of all, and she'd jump up on the bed and flop her legs over me (or push her back against my side), and she'd doze as I did. Sometimes, though, she'd kick her legs a little and growl, and I knew she was running a race in her dream. I wondered if she won until I realized, hey, what's the point of dreaming if you *don't* win?

I'd thought long ago about you only need a few seconds to dream what seems to be hours of action, and the ideas intersected here in "The Speed of Dreams." All I needed was a character in the right emotional state for whom dream-time-scrunch research would be most important, and the story essentially fell together.

Soon after its publication, however, Patti passed away. We had a great day before she did: one last walk, one last nap. She stood up to follow me from my writing table and simply collapsed for the last time. I'm not sure how I feel about her final act being one to follow me, but I'm glad I was there so she could hear my voice as she ran off to her dream races forever.

I suspect she wins them all.

Originally appeared in the March 2010 issue of Asimov's Science Fiction.

Nora's Thing

I suppose at least one of these story notes should discuss the prevalence of deranged, vengeful, and/or magically-inclined women in my work. I don't have much of a defense except, you know, I like women like that: perceptive, attuned, wry, powerful, creative, committed. I like men like that, too, but we have plenty of those in our literature already.

Originally appeared in the May 2012 Drabblecast *podcast.*

Remembrance is Something Like a House

The closest I come these days to a paranormal belief is that places can store the emotional energy of what happens there. Yes, I know rationally that I'm probably projecting what I know onto a non-sentient jumble of boards and bricks, but there have been many times when I've entered a place and gotten a chill of instant revulsion. I've backed out of their doors, hands up, saying, "No, something went horribly wrong in there."

Of course, rationally, something bad has happened in every place. But I've unquestionably felt strange things in seemingly normal places, and I choose to believe that I'm attuned to what happened there instead of, you know, just a neurotic weirdo.

This story came about as my reflection of just how murder houses feel about the crimes that happen in them. I'm sure they would love only to apologize.

Originally appeared in the Interfictions 2 *anthology, 2009.*

Whit Carlton's Trespasser

Rednecks for me are like Martians for Ray Bradbury: strange quasi-magical beings that don't correspond to any plausible culture except as mirror reflections of the reader's. The Martians have majestic sandships gliding across the deserts of Mars, and the rednecks have battered green Chevy pickup trucks with FUQ IRAQ bumper stickers. They both grant us insight into what we lack: Martians are our missing attunement with love and wonder, and rednecks are our lost feral simplicity.

Or, more accurately, rednecks have always creeped me out and they're fun to write about.

Originally appeared in the January 2012 Drabblecast *podcast.*

We Were Wonder Scouts

It took me way too long to figure this out, but the Boy Scouts kind of suck.

I don't mean the individual Scouts (though, yeah, a lot of them from my troop were cretins). I mean the organization as a whole—resisting as it does any kind of moral reflection or change, and perhaps even the very idea of it—encouraging an unquestioning obedience to fixed principles.

Now, I was desperate to join as a kid because I had my father's 1963 Boy Scout Handbook full of cheerful illustrations of perfect burgers sizzling in a pan, crisp green tents circled among the trees, stalwart young men doing good in the community. The book was all about adventure and heroism, honing yourself against the whetstone of nature.

When I joined for real, it was mostly a bunch of kids making farting noises with their armpits and calling each other gay. I was the only one who took it seriously...so much so, in fact, that they made fun of me for following the very letter of that handbook.

It took me many years (and some reading of Algernon Blackwood) to realize that what I really wanted was a sublime experience in the woods. I wanted to scrape against something deep and primal, to see something wondrous. I wanted to camp on a little island in the Danube and suspect that the willows were skulking around me.

Instead, I got a concussion when one kid shoved me off a mound of dirt and I hit my head on a rock.

So I thought about what I really wanted as a kid, and the Wonder Scouts came to mind. I wondered who would create such an organization and who would join it, and "We Were Wonder Scouts" more or less came together from that.

I like to think that I'm a real life Wonder Scout, and that this book is one of our organization's manuals. I hope you'll join us; unlike some OTHER organizations I can name, we accept gays and girls and anybody else who wants to see the behind the realness of things.

Originally appeared in the August 2011 issue of Asimov's Science Fiction.

Singularity Knocks

Many technology and science fiction writers, not to mention their readers and fans, look forward to a magical moment in the relatively near future when our computing technology exceeds our intelligence and a revolutionary new system of life arises. This moment is called the Singularity (or, less charitably, the rapture of the nerds). We will all be uploaded to computers and live out lives of fantasy and intellectual development.

I challenge anyone who believes that the human race is on the cusp of anything so wondrous to visit a Wal-Mart.

One of the funny things about the Singularity is that you don't often read about people discussing what to do with the folks who don't want the shiny new future. Do you leave them outside the computer to die or wreak mayhem? Do you suck them in unwillingly and hope they'll adjust?

It's the fundamental question of all societies, really: what do you do with the assholes?

I've always wondered what it would be like to be faced with the decision of shucking off my mortal body and going off to live as a pattern of electrons. I've wondered even more what Wal-Mart shoppers might do.

Originally appeared in the January 2012 Drabblecast *podcast.*

A Chamber to be Haunted

Of the many insane ideas I've had for alternate careers (lawyer, detective, programmer, counselor, middle manager), one I've never considered was anything to do with sales. Though my day job right now is training sales agents in insurance products, I don't have anything approaching the social courage to wheedle people to buy things.

Which is probably not that good for my career in our Internet-enabled buy-me culture.

If I did have to sell things, I'd want to sell houses because I love them, including all of their history, and I'd certainly specialize in stigmatized properties. Someone has to put a better spin on horror, right? That's what my whole childhood trained me to do.

Original to this collection.

She Shells

I am a certified diver, but I have to admit that water with living things in it scares the hell out of me. Why? Because ever since our betrayal from the primordial sea to the land, the creatures we have left behind have wanted nothing more than to wreak their awful vengeance on us.

Or so I imagine every time a tendril of seaweed—or a wisp of hair—curls around my ankle in the water.

Original to this collection.

Prudenter to Dream

I have no business being a parent for a variety of reasons, but the one that comes most easily to mind is that they scare me. They're shifty and unpredictable, a little like drunks, and I never quite know what to DO with them. Talk? Play? Ignore? It's all very confusing.

Several years ago, I visited my family in Gainesville at my sister's house for my niece's birthday. We all swam in the pool having a grand time. Then it occurred to me that I couldn't remember how old the birthday girl was. So I asked her and she told me.

I didn't like acknowledging that I didn't know that, so to save face, I replied, "Oh, you only think you're nine. Actually, you're forty years old and dreaming about your ninth birthday."

The look on her face as she processed that flickered between amazement and sadness. Where did all those memories in between go?

It wasn't a big leap to wonder WHY someone would want to dream about his or her ninth birthday instead of facing reality, and this story was the result.

Original to this collection.

Mom in the Misted Lands

I've been married twice and divorced twice, and I regret one of each. Even more, I regret that my desire for life to be an epic story often leads me to self-delusion: I've fought people for my soul who might not have been fighting back. There have been just enough who have, though, that it is sometimes hard to tell the difference.

I think this story is my way of saying I'm sorry for the times I failed to see the epic in others.

Original to this collection.

The Ghost Factory

A curiously large number of people in my life have been psychologists or social workers, largely because my parents and their associates tend to be people who attended school in the 60s and 70s when it was thought that we could plausibly fix the world by fixing the people in it.

Their experiences are almost all the same: they are like Ishmael clinging to Queequeg's coffin after the sinking of the Pequod, stunned into sublime awe by the sheer power and persistence of an ocean of human neurosis. Some people cannot be changed but merely survived.

I even flirted for a time with a degree in psychology, but I was afraid I'd have to be honest in my application letter and explain that I just wanted to study it to see how spectacularly fucked up people could be. I suspect that's what attracted my father to the profession, and this story is my extended meditation on just what kind of counselor he had to have been: the best and worst thing to happen to so many of the people in his charge.

Originally appeared in the October/November 2012 issue of Asimov's Science Fiction.

Burying the Hatchets

Yeah, I'm a big softy sometimes, and I believe in the redemptive power of weirdness. And when you think about it, weirdness is really just clouded cause and effect; if we don't know the variables that yielded a result, sometimes the only thing to do is try them all together again.

Was it my new watch or my anti-anxiety medication that helped me make a good impression at that interview? Eh, better try them both.

The great thing about magic, though, is that all of those variables might be doing good in ways you don't realize—as the kids in this story discover.

Original to this collection.

Universicule

Oh, poor Deconstruction: you are such an amusing target.

As a student of critical theory in the late 80s and early 90s, I was beset by all too many classes in the intrinsic conflicts of language, the deterministic effect of words upon thought, the undermining quality of false oppositions, the gender-determinism of Romance languages, the imperialistic quality of literature, the fractured and liminal spaces between...

I just wanted to be an Indiana Jones of books, okay? I wanted to find lost manuscripts, figure out what the hell Samuel Johnson had that made him stutter and quiver, and then quietly lecture in my corduroy jacket with the elbow patches. Was that too much to ask?

Yet I'll admit that I enjoyed all of that critical theory. For one thing, some of it is actually true. For another, even when it isn't true, it gives you that endorphin rush of an argument that trumps all other arguments: "You're disagreeing with me because you're too invested in the system of language qua language, man." And for a third, all that folding back and forth of language reminded me of programming, coaxing meaning out of meaninglessness.

So every so often, I write a story about literary theorists living their consequences of their theories. Like this one.

Original to this collection.

About the Author

Will Ludwigsen's fiction has appeared in *Alfred Hitchcock's Mystery Magazine*, *Asimov's Science Fiction*, *Weird Tales*, *Strange Horizons*, and many other magazines. His first collection of short fiction, *Cthulhu Fhtagn, Baby! and Other Cosmic Insolence*, appeared in 2007. A 2011 MFA graduate from the University of Southern Maine's Stonecoast program in popular fiction, he teaches creative writing at the University of North Florida.

He resides in Jacksonville, Florida, with writer Aimee Payne.

CPSIA information can be obtained at www.ICGtesting.com
Printed in the USA
LVOW080647190213

320679LV00003B/9/P